First published by Elizabeth's Group 2024

Copyright 2024 by Susan Munro

All rights reserved. No part of this publication may be reproduced, stored or transmitted in any form or by any means, electronic, mechanical, photocopying, recording, scanning, or otherwise without written permission from the publisher. It is illegal to copy this book, post it to a website, or distribute it by any other means without permission.

Susan Munro asserts the moral right to be identified as the author of this work.

Susan Munro has no responsibility for the persistence or accuracy of URLs for external or third-party Websites referred to in this publication and does not guarantee that any content on such Websites is, or will remain, accurate or appropriate.

This book is a work of fiction based on the actual life of Elizabeth Wolstenholme Elmy, a pioneer of the women's movement. The dialogues and character depictions are all from the imagination of the author, whilst the achievements and situations depicted are actual facts.

First edition

ISBN: 978-1-0687732-0-4

Justice is a Woman
The Wolstenholme Elmy Story

SUSAN MUNRO

*Enjoy!
Sue
xxx*

Elizabeth Wolstenholme Elmy
1833 - 1918

DEDICATION

This book is dedicated to my soulmate, my very own Ben.
Without his constant support and belief in my abilities,
the statue and this book would never have happened.

With all my love to

Peter Ian Munro

PROLOGUE

It was on International Women's Day 2018 that I first heard the name, Elizabeth Wolstenholme Elmy and since then I have been fascinated by the life and times of this amazing woman. When I first heard of her, she had been lost for many years in the dark corners of history but rediscovered and extensively studied by Dr Maureen Wright, to whom I owe a debt of gratitude for her forensic work and the writing of her biography (Elizabeth Wolstenholme Elmy and the Victorian Feminist Movement: The biography of an insurgent woman).

Elizabeth's life was a life of conflict and struggle, a fight for justice for women and girls that spanned the 19th and 20th Century. A fight that has gone down in history as the fight for the vote, but the vote was just one of many battles that Elizabeth fought. Domestic violence, marital rape, reproductive rights, property rights and education for women and girls are numbered on the long list of her campaigns and victories. She was even the animal rights advocate of her age with her anti-vivisection campaigns.

Elizabeth's story and the fact that she had been so far in advance of her age and that she had, in some cases, been deliberately written out of the history of the women's movement, propelled me into action. The sheer unfairness of the situation; all she had done, sacrificed and achieved, all forgotten. It made me angry beyond words and I decided to do something about it.

I called a meeting of people who thought likewise, and we became Elizabeth's Group a small charity whose sole purpose was to get Elizabeth recognised, remembered and honoured for all her achievements. Together we campaigned "Elizabeth Style" and raised the funds to commission a statue of her to be erected on International Women's Day 2022, four years later.

The statue "Our Elizabeth" was created by Hazel Reeves and unveiled by Lady Hale of Richmond on 8th March 2022 and now stands proudly in Congleton in Cheshire where she lived, campaigned and taught for over 54 years.

This book attempts to tell a story based on her life and times, as I imagine it to be.

Susan Munro
Chair
Elizabeth's Group

CONTENTS

		PAGE
PART ONE	**The Early Years - 1850 – 1867**	
Chapter 1	A Day of Change	8
Chapter 2	Elizabeth Wolstenholme	13
Chapter 3	Life at Fulneck	22
Chapter 4	Home Again	27
Chapter 5	Independence	33
Chapter 6	Hermitage Grange	37
Chapter 7	Roe Green Again	47
Chapter 8	The Grange School Boothstown	50
Chapter 9	Contagious Diseases	53
Chapter 10	Free Love	59
PART TWO	**Branching Out - 1867 - 1890**	
Chapter 11	Time for Change	63
Chapter 12	Benjamin John Elmy	66
Chapter 13	Moody Hall 1867	70
Chapter 14	The Courtship	75
Chapter 15	Christmas at Moody Hall 1868	84
Chapter 16	Life in the Fast Lane	91
Chapter 17	Battles and Disappointments	95
Chapter 18	The Birth	104
Chapter 19	The Victor	110
Chapter 20	Salford Mill	114
Chapter 21	A Meeting of Importance	117
Chapter 22	Frank Wolstenholme Elmy	123
Chapter 23	The Years Roll On	125
Chapter 24	Treachery and Revenge	132
PART THREE	**Fame and Notoriety - 1890 - 1918**	
Chapter 25	Clitheroe Lancashire February 1890	138
Chapter 26	The Women's Emancipation Union	145
Chapter 27	The Boer War	150
Chapter 28	Women's Social Political Union 1903	155
Chapter 29	Treacherous Men and Richard 1 1906	157
Chapter 30	Ben's Death 1907	162
Chapter 31	Life Without Ben	166
Chapter 32	Treacherous Women and Emmeline Pankhurst	168
Chapter 33	William T. Stead 1912	171
Chapter 34	The Women's Suffrage March Summer 1913	179
Chapter 35	The Archive	184
Chapter 36	The End of All Things 1918	189

The Song of the Insurgent Women

We come! We are here at last!
Sisters, ye waited long.
But the cold dark night is past,
And the day breaks clear and strong.

What are the gifts we bring?
Hope, in the place of despair,
Truth in everything,
And justice everywhere.

These are the gifts we bring,
And their magical powers shall last
Till the beast in man is slain,
And man is Man at last.

Then Love, undying Love
Shall shape the old work anew,
Brighter than heaven above,
Fresher than morning dew.

And our beautiful human life,
Free from all sad annoy,
No space for empty strife,
Shall be charged to the full with joy.

We come! We are here at last!
Sisters, ye waited long.
And the cold dark night is past,
And the day breaks clear and strong.

Elizabeth Wolstenholme-Elmy
(14th November 1906)

PART ONE

The Early Years
1850 – 1867

CHAPTER 1
A Day of Change

Thwack!

The cane whizzed down and landed upon the upturned palms of a tiny 12-year-old girl. It was wielded with force by her father the Reverend Joseph Wolstenholme, and it had become a regular occurrence over the preceding year. Ever since the wedding of her cousin Sybil, after which she had started to ask the sort of questions that he considered no respectable young girl should ask.

Thwack! It landed a second time. "A married woman vows to obey her husband because she belongs to him."

Thwack! A third lash. "A young girl belongs to her father until such time as he gives her in marriage."

Thwack! "It is the Christian way and ordained by God himself."

Thwack! "*The wife hath not power of her own body, but the husband* "1 Cor 7:4." he bellowed.

Thwack! "Now Elizabeth, leave my sight and may I suggest you spend the afternoon reading the Holy Scripture and not the ramblings of Mary Wollstonecraft. No decent, God-fearing young female should ever read that disgusting woman's writings. The devil finds work for idle hands Elizabeth and fills the silly, empty minds of disobedient young girls with claptrap. You will get yourself into serious trouble if you continue on this path young lady."

Elizabeth stood before her father, arms outstretched, and palms turned up. Her eyes had been fastened to his throughout the whole ordeal. She had not blinked nor had her face shown any sign of the pain he inflicted. Her eyes remained fixed on his and her stiff, defiant little body had completed almost a quarter turn before she pulled them reluctantly away and walked stiffly toward his study door. Slowly she opened it and stepping out into the hall, she closed it softly behind her.

She took two paces into the hall and then, and only then did she squeeze her eyes closed as two small tears escaped and trickled down her cheeks. She squeezed her hands closed and then then opened them again. She repeated the action several times in an attempt to abate the exquisite pain the cane had inflicted and then tucked them into her armpits for a few seconds as she rocked gently back and forth. Quickly wiping away her tears, she rubbed her palms on her thighs as the pain lessened slightly and turned instead to pins and needles with an underlying throb.

She crossed the hall and entered the kitchen where cook concerned, looked up from her baking and asked, "are you alright Miss Elizabeth?"

"Perfectly, thank you cook," she said as she forced a bright smile across her face.

She could hear the dog outside, barking and howling in his misery so she crossed to the window and looked out. There he was in his usual place, chained to his kennel. He had spent almost every day of his sad life there. He was thrown scraps now and again, but it wasn't enough, he was malnourished, aggressive and resentful of any human who went near him.

Driven mad by the chain that bound him, he howled out his misery by day and by night, in blistering sun and icy-cold snow. There was only one human he trusted and that was Elizabeth. She sneaked him treats and fed him when she could.

She had tried to plead his case with her father, but her father had said. *"A righteous man regardeth the life of his beast: but the tender mercies of the wicked are cruelty.* Proverbs 12:10. It is a dog Elizabeth, it has a job, if it does it well it gets fed if it doesn't earn its keep it gets replaced. The Lord gave man dominion over every living creature."

She went through the back door and crossed the yard and Theodore, the name she had given him and only she ever used, stopped the noise immediately, concertinaed up his body, put his ears back and swung his heavy tail from side to side in excitement and pleasure. She fell to her knees in front of him and put her arms around his neck. She ran her poor, hurting hands through the warm fur on his back to ease the pain and pressed her face into his neck, fighting back the tears. After a while, she sat upright and looked into the dog's eyes. He stared back at her in mutual misery.

"Poor Theodore, poor boy, we are both owned by my father, both of us can do nothing but obey his every command or we will be punished. That's the way it is, that's the law of this land; we are both bound by chains. I hate it that I have to submit to the will of my father, I hate it that Joseph gets to go to school whilst I can only look forward to a life of servitude and enforced motherhood and I hate it that I cannot help you."

Theodore licked her face, his sensitive, intelligent eyes reaching out to her. Elizabeth felt a deep, deep anger welling up inside her. It was the anger she felt when she read Mary's book, the anger she had felt at Sybil's wedding when she heard her uncle 'give her away' and Sybil submit and take the vow to 'obey' her new husband. It was the anger she felt when Theodore was shouted at or kicked or left out in the snow or the sun without food and water and suddenly, suddenly she knew, she was going to change things. She was going to take the knowledge that Mary had given her and fight for autonomy for herself and other girls and women.

She was never going to marry, why should she give up all rights and become a chattel to some man who was probably only marrying her for her money? She was never going to capitulate and 'obey' no, she was going to stand on Mary's shoulders and make real, lasting change happen.

Elizabeth looked at Theodore. "There is no God Teddy or if there is then he is a cane-wielding, tyrant like my father." She drew in a deep breath and made a decision. "I can't change much for myself at the moment, but I can change things for you right now." Rising quickly to her feet, she went back into the kitchen and into the scullery. She took the rope that hung at the back of the door and went back to the dog. She released his chain, replaced it with the rope, and led the dog across the yard and through the gate out into the ginnel beyond.

The dog could not believe what was happening to him. As they came out of the end of the ginnel and onto the green, he suddenly realised what was taking place and took off at great speed pulling the light-weight girl behind him. She threw back her head and laughed as he pulled her after him, skirts flapping and hair flying in the wind.

She travelled across the green and through the houses, past her father's chapel and out onto the common land at Roe Green. Onwards and onwards, they ran until Elizabeth, lacking the breath to continue, pulled him to a stop. She sat down on the grass and looked around her taking in the beauty of the natural world. She looked again at Theodore's face and again he returned her stare.

"Theodore; Teddy" she gently pulled off the rope and said, "Go free Ted, go free little dog."

She watched him as he set off running free, round and round he ran, down to the beck where he drank deeply and paddled a while before climbing out the other side and running up the hill away from her.

She didn't know what his fate would be. He was likely to be shot by a farmer or attacked by other dogs. She hoped that maybe he could catch a rabbit or two and live out the rest of his life in wild freedom. Or maybe he would reach the Gin Pit Village at Astley and be befriended by a friendly mining family, but anyway he was now free.

As she watched him go, she knew her father would punish her again and replace him with another poor puppy who he would keep in chains to guard his property; at least sweet, loving Theodore would be free of his misery.

She watched him go up the hill to the very top and then he turned and looked back. He sniffed the air and looked all around. He sat down and seemed to spend some time deliberating the situation. Standing again he stared at her across the distance. She could hardly see him now, but he still had her fixed in his vision.

Slowly, he began to move, he didn't seem to know what to do but suddenly he seemed to make up his mind and he started back towards her. He gathered speed as he cleared the beck for the second time and hurled himself at her in a paroxysm of mad, doggy happiness.

Elizabeth looked at him and realised that he had returned to her, because he loved her and because the few drops of human kindness that she gave him were the only sure thing in his sad, miserable life. He knew he had nowhere else to go, so he returned to the awful prison that was the only life he knew.

Elizabeth Wolstenholme was to remember this day for the rest of her life. Would remember it as a defining moment. The moment when her stubborn tenacity was born, and her mind became set. This was the day that gave her life meaning.

In the days that followed as her painful hands slowly healed, her mind became more and more set as she thought through her options and made her first tentative plans.

CHAPTER 2
Elizabeth Wolstenholme

Elizabeth

I was born in 1833; it was not a good time to be a girl. We are only expected to produce the next generation, actively discouraged from any activity deemed "unladylike" and denied an education simply because we are of the female sex. I was never one to complain, oh no not Elizabeth Wolstenholme, I just get my head down and get on with the job, but this situation is making me extremely angry.

My father, the much-respected Reverend Joseph Wolstenholme has been trying for the last 15 years to turn me into a good, obedient Christian daughter, but I quickly realised that his religion and his God were merely tools to control people. He believes implicitly I am sure, but I certainly do not. I have heard him preach on so many occasions and although I stand in awe of. his skills of oratory, his message does not stand up to any close scrutiny. He has tried every trick in his book to make me think differently. Finally resorting to violence, quoting his Bible to justify the act. What he didn't realise is that rather than knocking his God into me, as was his want, he was actually knocking his God, and any other for that matter, completely and utterly out of me.

I took it all; every caning every harsh word, every enforced restriction on my liberty or loathsome task he compelled me to undertake as punishment, I took it all and remained silent or put forward a reasoned argument. The latter usually ended in another caning. Like the time I asked him why the Bible contradicted itself and he said it didn't.

"The Holy Bible is wholly true" he had railed.

I pointed out that Matthew's Gospel says seven loaves and five fish for the feeding of four thousand, whilst the other Gospels say five loaves and two fish fed five thousand. He went an exquisite shade of red on that occasion for it is there, in black and white in his book.

I shouldn't laugh, his unwavering belief in the truth of the Bible leads him to the idea that females have smaller brains than males, and are lesser creatures, the chattels of men, not individual, free-thinking people in their own right. For this reason, he has always refused me an education whilst shelling out a fortune to educate Joseph Junior, my *brother: how unfair is that?*

However, all that is in the past now for my father is dead! Do I feel sad? Yes, I do as for all his faults, he was my father and did his best, within his limited knowledge and the constraints of his suffocating religion.

I often wonder if things would have been different had my mother lived, but she died at my birth, or very soon thereafter so was not around to fight my corner and plead my case. I do have my stepmother Mary, but she is a weak sort of person who accepts her lot in life stoically and would certainly not put herself in the line of fire to help my cause. Of course, I am falling into the trap of thinking that my mother would have been like me strong and resolute.

We should not expect much of the dead for they are dead and cannot speak or act for themselves, and we become sentimental in our grief and give them traits and thought processes they were unlikely to have had in life, and certainly not in death.

People have said "Your mother would be disgusted at you" or "your mother would be so proud."

I cry nonsense! You cannot know these things for she has no opinion now, she is dead and gone, her time is over and done and we the living, must plough our own furrow.

Back to the sad demise of my father: it sets me a dilemma. I am now 15 years of age, at the mercy of my Uncle George and my grandfather who are now my legal guardians and under the law of this land, I am their property.

I must plan my strategy well: I see my father's death as an opportunity for me to plead my case with my grandfather, he is a horse of a different sort; not as harsh or unbending as my father and he knows how much I want to be educated and independent. I hope he feels some sympathy. I know he sees it as a silly dream, but if I can just persuade him to allow me a few years at a decent school I could still further my education.

However, there is Uncle George who is very much of the old school, very like father: he will see me as a millstone round his neck and will be looking to off-load me into wedlock as soon as possible. I am facing the fight of my life with these two gentlemen.

****

The Funeral

She cut a strange figure, stood by the graveside, so tiny and swathed in black crepe. Her stepmother and her brother stood to her right and across the open grave stood her Uncle George, her grandfather and grandmother. She watched as her grandfather threw a handful of soil onto her father's coffin followed by her uncle and then her brother. Her stepmother and grandmother threw next leaving her, last in the hierarchy to do the same. She stooped to pick up a handful of soil and dropped it down the hole where it landed with an echoing thud onto the coffin lid. She stood motionless taking in the awfulness of the moment. It did not feel right to be throwing earth at her father, but that was what the occasion required her to do, and she would have been judged had she followed her feelings and refused to take part in their ritual.

His departure from this life had been a difficult and harrowing affair for all concerned. He had been weak and very confused; refused all ministrations from poor Mary her stepmother insisting unfairly, that she was trying to kill him! He had demanded that only Elizabeth should tend to his needs. Thus, she found herself acting as chief nurse, caring for him round the clock. She kept quiet about the unfairness of the situation. it was a waste of time to point out that Joseph should at least be sharing the task. She knew that as the daughter it fell to her and she had no argument that she could use that would not make her look ungrateful and unloving, so she had worked on in silence until his death four days ago.

When the funeral party began to break away from the churchyard, she followed them as they walked toward the rectory and the funeral tea which was waiting. Her heart was heavy because she knew she was in for yet another argument. She had told her grandfather that she wanted to go to school and had even chosen the one she wanted, Fulneck Moravian School in Leeds. She had researched their curriculum and it suited her very well; she felt that the deeply religious, Quaker ethos would appeal to their puritanical mindset and perhaps influence their decision. Most of all she knew that Fulneck treated boys and girls the same and encouraged girls to consider themselves equal to men and to act accordingly, which suited her down to the ground.

She suspected that Uncle George had plans to marry her off to get her off his hands and therefore off his conscience, but she wanted the dowry money to be spent on her education instead of her imprisonment. She knew she had the fight of her life ahead and that it would be an important point in her life. Her father may have been very traditional and very religious, but he would never force her to marry someone she had never met; Uncle George on the other hand, was a different kettle of fish. She followed the funeral party through the garden gate and in through the front door.

Jane was waiting in the parlour with tea and an assortment of sandwiches and cakes. Elizabeth nibbled on a sandwich and drank a cup of tea, and all the time knew that Uncle George and her grandfather were in her father's study talking, and the topic of their conversation was her future.

"Cheer up old girl, it might never happen." She turned to face Joseph her brother.

"I think it already has" she retorted.

"It'll all be alright in the end Elizabeth. I know you want to study and it's highly commendable but, is the idea of a life as a wife and mother really that abhorrent?"

He made a silly face and Elizabeth fought the over-powering desire to punch it! Just as she was about to verbally attack him the study door opened and her grandfather crossed the hallway, put his head around the parlour door and spoke "Elizabeth, will you join us in the study please?"

She pulled herself up to her fullest height, pulled her shoulders back and with her head proudly in the air, she walked slowly out of the room, across the hall and into the study.

George was standing looking out of the window and as she entered, he turned and smiled grotesquely at her.

"Elizabeth, I am so sorry to be here under these terrible circumstances, but I think you will agree that we need to quickly sort out your future arrangements. You will no doubt be delighted to hear that I have some excellent news for you. I have arranged for you to be married to a charming young man from a good, well-connected family. His name is Charles Goodridge, and I am settling a £300 dowry on you upon your marriage, which will be shortly after you turn 16 later this year. In the meantime, your grandfather has agreed that you can stay in his house as his guest. Now what do you say to that?"

Elizabeth was taken aback by his manner; he was not usually a jovial sort of person. She knew it was an act put on for her benefit. She was being patronised and treated like a child and she resented it. She did not return his smile.

"Thank you, Sir, I appreciate your time and effort on my behalf but, no thank you. I do not want to marry someone I have never met; indeed, I do not want to marry at all. I want to go to Fulneck, and I intend to be a teacher and be financially independent." Growing earnest now she continued, "Uncle that £300 would pay for my studies which will enable me to live independently and consequently I will no longer be a burden to you. I am not an animal that can be bought and sold. I do not wish to appear ungrateful but surely it is my right to have control over my own destiny, nay my own body?" She stared into his face imploringly and refused to break her gaze.

The colour drained from George's face, and he began to splutter "You, you, you, this is unbelievable, you ridiculous girl, whoever heard of such a suggestion. You will never be able to earn enough money to be independent, you are a woman, and respectable women just do not do that kind of thing. No, no, no you will do as you are told and marry into the Goodridge Family, believe me, you will have a happy life. I would have a clear conscience if you married Charles."

"No sir, you cannot make me marry against my will and I will not marry. Grandfather please be fair to me; you know how much I want this. Joseph has had a first-rate education paid for by yourself and I have had so very little. Please I beg of you, give me my chance, let me go to Fulneck."

"Leave the room" yelled George, "get out of my sight you disgraceful creature."

Elizabeth walked out and down the passage to the kitchen. She could see and hear the staff busily washing cups and plates and getting ready for the next stage of the proceedings. She stood still for a moment composing herself and then she turned and walked back to the parlour. Some of the guests had already gone and she stood for a while by the doorway with Joseph and said goodbye to the rest as they left the house.

When she was alone with her brother and her stepmother she walked across the room and sitting next to Mary took her hand and said "There, there mother the ordeal is over now. Tomorrow is a new day, and we must find the strength to face whatever it brings. Let us hope it brings better luck than we have had of late."

Mary dissolved into a paroxysm of weeping and Elizabeth placed her arms around her shoulders and let her weep, she knew that this was the time, now that the funeral proceedings were over, the formalities out of the way when Mary could indulge her emotions.

"How did it go old girl?" Joseph asked in a hushed voice.

"Very ill; they want to marry me off to some man I have never met and are paying him to do so. I may have to leave and try to make it on my own."

"But Elizabeth there is only ruin out there for a penniless young girl. The world is a hard enough place for married women, single, unsupported women are destined for a life of destitution. Please think carefully before you make such a decision."

"Could I not come to you in Oxford? Just for a short time until I sort myself out. Surely you won't let me be sold off like this?" Elizabeth was panicking now.

Joseph looked troubled as he replied. "Be calm sister, of course you could come to me for a season, but I really don't know how you can "sort yourself out" I don't think there are opportunities for that."

There was a moment of realisation and then she returned her attention to her stepmother who was still sobbing but in a quiet dignified way. She tightened her arms around her and rocked her gently back and forth in mutual misery.

An hour later her Uncle George left the study, took his coat and hat from the hall stand and left the house. Stood at the window she watched him go round the back of the house and then shortly afterwards, reappear mounted on his horse. He passed the window and then turned right up the high street and disappeared from view.

She knew some sort of decision had been made and that her grandfather was the one who would tell her the outcome. She knew that she was either going to Fulneck or leaving the family forever, but not as a wife, for she would never marry, but what could a 15-year-old girl do alone in the world, powerless and without protection?

****

Her grandfather kept her waiting a full week; he left her in anxious suspense. It was a long week during which she suffered agonies imagining a wedding to this unknown man, but inevitably she was called into the study.

"George and I have had a difference of opinion. He is convinced that marriage to Charles Goodridge is the best and only way forward for you and that this arranged marriage would cure you of the strange notions you have. I on the other hand am of the opposite opinion. I know you well Elizabeth and I know your desire for education runs deep and is heartfelt. Therefore, I have decided to override your uncle's decision and I have enrolled you at Fulneck.

I hope you will be very happy and make the most of your opportunity. I have given a budget of £200 which should allow you two years and I suggest you make the most of it for there will be no more beyond that. Upon your return, we will again discuss your future and the possibility of a suitable marriage. Go well Elizabeth."

Elizabeth couldn't believe her ears, her eyes brimmed with tears of relief, as she rushed forward and embraced her grandfather.

"Oh, Grandpa thank you, thank you so much. I knew you would never let me down."

Taking hold of her arms, he pushed against her embrace and held her to arm's length. Giving her a little shake he began earnestly "Elizabeth, it is not that George doesn't love you he just wants to do the best by you.

He wants to see you safe and settled into a good life. He sees this marriage as a great opportunity and can't understand why a girl like yourself wouldn't jump at the chance. Don't be too hard on him."

She looked into his eyes and replied "I am not a grudge-bearer Grandpa, I have what I wanted, and I am not about to make myself bitter by hatred. But now I need to plan my wardrobe and my travel arrangements. May I be excused?"

Her grandfather nodded and she turned to leave but reaching the door she turned and looked towards the old man and was overcome with gratitude and love. "Thank you, thank you Grandpa you have been the one shining star in my life."

The old man looked startled and then threw back his head and laughed as she opened the door to leave.

Joseph and Mary looked up in amazement at the unusual sound of Richard Clarke's laughter and were delighted to see an excited Elizabeth rushing across the hall to the morning room where they sat.

"I'm going to Fulneck, I'm going to Fulneck." She clapped her hands and skipped around the room.

"Bravo wonderful news" shouted Joseph rising to his feet and hugging her.

Mary Wolstenholme completely taken aback, remained silent for several seconds before she let out a great breath of air. "We'd better get planning for your departure Elizabeth, I cannot say you haven't earned this, but I can say that you will be greatly missed and not in the least by me. Good luck my lovely girl I am so pleased for you; you truly deserve this."

Back in the study Richard Clarke sat in the battered old chair and thought about the future. He couldn't understand how he was here, still alive when his daughter, son-in-law and one grandchild were dead. He loved Elizabeth and had enjoyed the years she had been a small baby and toddler in his house following her mother's death; of all his grandchildren she was the brightest. If only she had been a boy, she could have taken over the world, he mused. Now here she was so absolutely besotted with the idea of going away to school. She will have to marry soon though, he knew that, or die an "Old Maid" which was the worst fate he could think of for a young woman.

Elizabeth

Well, I can hardly believe it! I am victorious; I'm going to Fulneck. You should have seen Joseph's face when I told him. He looked shocked to the core, but I think he was pleased for me, even if it does mean there's less money to fund his university fees. I do not believe he would be so selfish as to resent the money being spent, for he is one of the few people in my family that I feel loves me and understands how I feel about the unfairness of my plight.

I am going to make the best of my time at Fulneck, I intend to enjoy every single minute I have there. It has been such a hard battle, and the victory is sweet; I simply must get everything I can out of my time there. Just two short years Grandpa said, well I will be so brilliantly successful that they will give me longer. They will not be able to refuse. I shall work solidly and be top of the class in all subjects; I will make them see that I must be allowed to continue my studies. I shall be the most productive scholar in the history of the school and win all prizes. Then they will be forced to admit that I need to be allowed to continue my studies. Oh, how happy I am, how absolutely and completely ecstatic, hurrah I'm going to Fulneck.

CHAPTER 3
Life at Fulneck

Heart like a war drum Elizabeth boarded the train for Leeds. She was accompanied by her grandmother's personal maid Doris Burns, who was being trusted to chaperone her to Fulneck. Doris was enjoying her freedom and the trip to Leeds. She saw it as a jolly holiday and chatted on and on pointing out interesting sights through the train window. Her infectious excitement added to her own feelings of liberation. This is it, the day she had dreamed of for so long. She had seen pictures of the school of course, but she could not imagine what living there would be like.

She was soon to find that life at school fulfilled all her hopes and dreams. Fulneck encouraged and challenged its young women to pursue their talents to the full. It suited Elizabeth down to the ground and she blossomed under the tutelage of this prestigious establishment. Fulneck reinforced for her the importance of education and built within her the steadfastness she required to carry out the amazing work she was destined to undertake.

Oh, those Halcyon Days at Fulneck, they suited the strong-willed Elizabeth perfectly by feeding her thirst for knowledge and encouraging her to consider herself equal to men. Her family indulged her in her education for the time she was at Fulneck just as Richard Clarke had promised and they paid extra fees for music and language lessons also.

Her days were full and always interesting. The bell rang at 6:00 am every morning and she was required to rise and dress as quickly as possible. As can be imagined during the winter this was not the most enjoyable part of her day, but she forged good, long-lasting friendships with the other girls and the camaraderie got them through the cold and frosty winter mornings. Once dressed the girls were off to an early breakfast and then their school day started properly.

Fulneck was housed in a beautiful building overlooking the Tong Valley and during the summer months the pupils would take nature rambles and picnics in the countryside and help with the growing of vegetables in the gardens. They would take their lessons on the sunlit terrace and all to the background accompaniment of the beautiful pipe organ that was housed in the church above their school; these were truly happy times for the young Elizabeth.

Elizabeth

The huge school clock is chiming in the hall, I can hear it as I fight through the layers of sleep and into total consciousness. As I surface a wave of happiness engulfs me as my senses take in my surroundings: the sight and sound of an awakening school. Agatha snores softly over the other side of the room, she's still in the Land of Nod, whilst far away the kitchen staff are noisily preparing breakfast, the bumps, and clangs sound sharp on the morning air.

I blow air from my lungs, and I see that it leaves my body in a cloud of vapour. It is really cold this morning so breakfast will be porridge, fruit and toast but first I must brave the lavatory and cold-water wash.

I shift my gaze to take in the end of my bed and can see my shawl draped across it ready for me to force my sleepy body into action. I mentally prepare myself for my morning ritual, for I like to have routines and things done in an orderly and correct manner. I will count to ten and on the tenth count, I will rise swiftly, grab the shawl and wrap it around me whilst hurrying for the lavatory. Eight, nine, ten and I'm off!

I hurry through my routine shivering from the cold as I dress. Other girls are up and about, some following my example, giggling as they dress in the early morning light. Others prolong the agony by grumbling and moving slowly through the process, trying to keep a shawl wrapped around them, uselessly trying to keep the cold out. Up and dressed, hair combed and looking smart, I am ready to start my day at Fulneck.

Fulneck how I love you. The battle I had to get here has been so worth it. I have been here for six months now and there hasn't been a day when I have not given thanks to the Universe for this wonderful opportunity. Just six months and already I know that teaching is the right path for me. I want to run a school for girls and help to fashion their lives to be free and complete citizens, living fulfilled and independent lives.

I have made so many friends, Alice, Agatha, Martha and Harriet are the closest as they share the dormitory with me. What good fun we have at bedtime. Getting to sleep is sometimes very difficult as Agatha is a terrible snorer and Alice seems to think throwing something at her across the pitch-black dormitory, will get her to be silent. It does not of course, it just makes a terrible noise and causes much laughter.

Morning finds us reluctant to wake and leave our beds, but it must be done or the housemistress Miss Barker, descends upon us with an angry visage. Nobody wants to get on the wrong side of Miss Barker, she rules with a rod of iron, and some say she is crossed with a tiger! It is all good-natured fun really, and even Miss Barker has been known to laugh at Alice's antics.

Last night, I discovered that naughty Alice had made me an "apple pie bed." My bottom sheet had been folded in half and tucked in, making a small envelope affair, with its opening appearing to be the top of the bed. It meant that when I attempted to get into my bed my feet wouldn't go further than halfway. After trying to get in for quite a while I heard Harriet and Agatha giggling in the darkness and realised my dilemma.

All things are sent to try us! I heard my father's voice clearly in my head, as I fumbled around in the dark trying to remake my bed. The girls seemed to treat me as some sort of hero for not castigating Alice and getting angry, but I had learned at an early age that anger is a negative emotion and achieves nothing whereas, keeping your head and facing up to things in a calm manner always gives you the upper hand. However, I have to admit, it was very funny and I did laugh myself once I was tucked up comfortably for the night.

"I will get you back Alice," I called through the darkness and the room dissolved into laughter.

The lessons themselves are interesting and I am learning so much, I always knew I would love it here, but it has surpassed all my expectations, and I am truly in paradise. Grandfather has given me a very generous allowance and has even paid extra for me to receive music and French tuition as well. He is keeping his part of the bargain we made but Uncle George does not write to me: he bears a grudge I fear. He does not take kindly to being bettered by a girl, but he is not the adversary my father was. I stood before his cane and his wrath many times and refused to acknowledge the pain: that was my only victory on those occasions; George is small fry compared with the Rev Joseph Wolstenholme.

*****

By the time her two years were up Elizabeth Wolstenholme had become a human dynamo, a courageous and passionate young woman who was determined to fulfil her potential and change the lives of women and girls for the better. She returned to Roe Green steadfast in the knowledge that the life she was to lead was a life of service and dedication.

As her time at Fulneck was drawing to an end, one of her school mistresses encouraged her to take the entrance examination for the newly established Bedford College and of course, Elizabeth passed with flying colours. She was bursting with pride and the mistress assured her that when she wrote to her grandfather, he would be so proud of her he would change his mind and allow her to remain in full-time education and take up the prized place at Bedford. Alas, this was not the case. Uncle George would not change his mind and stuck firmly to his guns, declaring that Elizabeth must return to Roe Green at the end of term and give up such silly ideas once and for all.

Therefore, a disappointed and resentful Elizabeth Wolstenholme left her beloved Fulneck and returned to the sooty, filth of Manchester. Heavy of heart she wondered just what life had in store for her next.

It was a sad party on her last night at Fulneck. Elizabeth and her friends held a candle-lit vigil. They sat around a dim candle until the early hours talking and pledging to always be friends and to always keep in touch.

Elizabeth was not the only one returning reluctantly home; Harriet and Alice were also terminating their education. These three young women pledged solemnly to never marry, to meet again whenever they could and to write to each other constantly never losing contact. They cried as if their hearts would break at the leaving of Fulneck and the fear of what their future in the big, wide world would hold.

When Uncle George arrived the next morning, he was bleary-eyed and had obviously enjoyed the delights of the Leeds nightlife the previous evening. He looked surly and not in the mood for conversation. He stood idly by as two small maids struggled to put Elizabeth's large trunk in the carriage.

Alice whispered in Elizabeth's ear. "Beware the demon drink" and Elizabeth giggled.

"Hurry Elizabeth there isn't time for girlish jangling, we have a train to catch." George bellowed, annoyed by the girls' giggling.

Elizabeth turned to her dear friends and hugged them both close. "I shall write my first letters tonight and I promise to write at least once a week from here in."

"Elizabeth! Hurry please we have no time to spare." called George crossly.

She hurried over to the cab and lifting her skirt she climbed daintily into her seat. George joined her and slammed the door. Elizabeth's face was fixed to the window as she watched Harriet, Alice and Fulneck grow smaller and smaller.

CHAPTER 4
Home Again

The huge steam engine gave out an ear-piercing whistle as they walked past it, and a huge hissing sound sent steam billowing out across the oily platform.

Walking through the acrid cloud Elizabeth followed the procession. Her uncle led the way, top hat on head, frockcoat billowing, walking cane in hand. Head in the air he sailed proudly down the platform followed closely by the porter, carrying Elizabeth's trunk on his shoulder. Elizabeth herself brought up the rear. A tiny figure, poke bonnet on head, dressed in her usual long, satin dress and her woollen topcoat, for the December morning had all the feel of the festive season; sharp and crisp.

Moving down the length of the train her uncle finally chose a suitable first-class carriage and opening the train door, he held it and indicated to Elizabeth to climb aboard. He assisted her ascent with a hand placed beneath her elbow. She crossed the carriage to sit by the window in order to give the porter room to manoeuvre her trunk onto the overhead luggage rack.

"Thank you, my man." George said pompously as he pulled a thruppenny bit from his waistcoat pocket and handed it to the porter who in return, sycophantically tugged the peak of his cap saying, "Thank you sir." Then turning his body slightly he looked to Elizabeth, silently repeated the cap gesture and nodded his head towards her. She quickly nodded in return and then turned away her gaze.

Although the morning was light with a pale, wintry sun, Elizabeth's heart was heavy and dark. The last thing she wanted was to return to Manchester with her uncle and she was angry and depressed. If only her grandfather and uncle had allowed her to take up the hard-earned place at Bedford College, but they claimed they had spent far too much money on a girl's education as it was and Joseph's school fees were becoming crippling as he moved higher up the academic ladder; his time at Oxford was very expensive.

She closed her eyes and thought of Adella Thorpe a girl in her class, whose parents saw her education as very important. She was their only child, but she had no interest in anything other than her pretty clothes and her silly hair. She could have screamed with the unfairness of the situation. Adella had also taken the exam for Bedford but failed miserably: nowhere near bright enough, her parent's money had gained her the opportunity to sit the exam. She was totally unmoved as she watched her distraught mother weep uncontrollably with the disappointment of her failure. Silly, silly Adella she had thought.

And then there was Joseph. What was she supposed to feel about him? She did love her brother, but it was so unfair that he had received all the family's education budget and more, whilst she had been given so very little; just these two, all too short years at Fulneck. If the family money was indeed limited, then surely it should have been halved equally between the two of them? The unfairness was wholly gender-based and she felt it deeply.

She leaned back into the seat, placed her head on the backrest, closed her eyes and inhaled deeply. She could smell the acrid smoke of the locomotive through the open window, and it felt like the smell of misery and doom.

Her eyes came open with a start as the engine screamed out a warning whistle and the whole train crashed and shook as it jerked into life. She could hear the guards slamming the doors closed above the thunderous engine noise and she watched the guard walk backwards up the platform, whistle in mouth, flag waving in his hand. The train shuddered again and began to move. Slowly at first, jerking and straining as it struggled to gain traction, and then it squealed another warning and rumbled out of the station.

She watched through the open window as it noisily gained speed and quickly made the outer edges of the city. She closed the window to keep out the smoky, cold air and then stood precariously staring out at the city's buildings receding into the distance.

Goodbye Leeds, you have been kind, I have been happy here. Thank you for having me, she said under her breath.

"Elizabeth! Sit down immediately, what are you thinking of? It's very dangerous to stand and unseemly for a young woman." George shook his head in disdain.

Her uncle's rebuke cut across her thoughts, and she obediently sat down into her seat for the journey back to Manchester.

Elizabeth

Well, this is a turn for the worse. However, I am stronger now and older, I will not allow the men in my family to dictate my life. I'm a human being and should have the same rights as they have, and I will not be treated like an object or a farm animal: I must prepare myself for the fight ahead.

I now know with absolute certainty what I want to do: I want to teach. Teaching is the only way I can have a modicum of financial independence and I must never marry as to marry would merely make me the chattel of my husband. I will never submit to that humiliation, never, never, never. I am a free woman a feme sole, and I will never be feme covert: no Gods, no masters, free to follow my own path in life.

So, Grandfather, so George let battle commence.

****

Back in the study at Roe Green, Grandfather was silent as George said, "Elizabeth your grandfather and I have been making plans for your future and this time there is to be no nonsense from you. It has not been as easy this time around as you are now two years older and in danger of being "left on the shelf" but I have secured an offer of marriage from Robert Harding Esq, a widower who owns several cotton mills in Lancashire and is very wealthy. He requires a mother for his six orphaned children. He thinks you will suit him very well and does not require a dowry to take you on. You will have a privileged life and will want for nothing." Dropping his voice a little he went on. "Incidentally, Mr Harding is 56 years old, so you may well find yourself a wealthy widow in due course."

Elizabeth was appalled and it showed on her face. She had thought herself prepared for this, but it was even more dreadful than she expected. To be married off to some old man was the worst possible scenario.

"No, no, no, no I will not marry, I will not be bought and sold like a farm animal. I am a human being and I have rights."

George was prepared this time. "Under the law of this land Elizabeth, you are my property, you are not actually free to choose what happens to you. I am responsible for you, and I will decide your future. Your Grandfather took pity on you two years ago and totally against my better judgement, you were indulged with your two years at Fulneck. That is now in the past and we need to secure a reasonable, safe future for you. You could be a wife and mother to two children by now if he hadn't indulged your preposterous ideas."

Richard Clarke spoke up "Now, now George least said about that the better" there was a note of anger in his voice. "Elizabeth, I told you at the time that you had two years and then you must marry. George and I have provided you with the two years agreed and now is the time for you to honour your side of that bargain. Don't make this any harder than it needs to be. It is time for you to toe the line and be the dutiful woman your family and society requires you to be."

"No, no, never!" She was in danger of shouting now, and she knew that wouldn't be pleasant, she could feel herself losing control. They were going to force her into a marriage of their convenience, and she didn't know how to stop it. Overwhelmed, Elizabeth took control of her emotions, drawing on her past experience when facing her father, she turned and walked gracefully and silently from the room slowly closing the door behind her. With as much dignity as she could muster, she went up the stairs to her room.

She was angry; the unfairness of it all was drowning her in despair. She felt trapped, afraid, and utterly miserable. She was in a panic and could not settle. She knew that they would send Mary to find her and try to talk her round so, leaving her room, she quickly and quietly descended the stairs, scooped up her hat and coat, and left the house.

Walking quickly down the main street, she slowed her pace as she entered the churchyard and moved automatically towards her father's grave. The dark, miserable day matched her dark, miserable mood as she stood reading the headstone.

R.I.P.
Rev JOSEPH WOLSTENHOLME

Why were you so closed to the idea of me being independent and having an education? It was exactly what you wanted for Joseph; why not for me? She shouted at him in her head, but of course, she received no reply. She stood and waited as the pounding in her head subsided and she regained some of her usual composure. After several minutes the extreme cold, striking up from the stone flags, compelled her to move.

She walked slowly to the rear of the church building where the grass had grown longer and was less well cared for. Here lay older graves, the ones whose descendants had joined them in the ranks, of the forgotten and whose graves were no longer lovingly tended.

As she wandered through the stones, she came across a huge plot devoid of gravestones and stood looking at it. She recognised immediately what it was; it was the paupers' grave. Somewhere in the back of her mind she had known it was here but had forgotten enough for it to take her by surprise.

She stepped off the path and stood in the middle of the plot. She thought of all the poor people beneath her feet. The ones who could not afford elaborate funerals, their names forgotten, their lives rendered meaningless. The victims of diseases they could not afford doctors to tend, nor medicines to relieve. The poor, uneducated, overworked, and starved people of Roe Green.

She thought of the women, those who like her mother, had died in childbirth, their babies buried in their arms, sometimes whilst still alive, and those murdered by jealous, cruel husbands. The plot was huge, so they numbered many hundreds, and this was just here in Roe Green a very small corner of Manchester. How many thousands must there be across the city, and how many millions across England as a whole?

She stood transfixed; the cold forgotten as their voices shouted out to her from the ground. Their bones wailed for attention; the world heard them not, but at that moment, in that freezing cold graveyard Elizabeth did. She felt all the injustice of their plight, all the pain of their condition. Those voiceless ones beneath her feet cried out for justice, and she alone heard them clearly.

But she heard other voices too, voices of other women, women very much alive, women suffering right now. Living breathing women like her, women at the mercy of men with no means of independent support.

Uneducated and hopeless women, forced to sell their bodies to feed their children.

And yet a third set of voices whispered on the cold morning wind; voices from the future, voices calling for equality and justice. At that moment her heart answered them, the words formed on her lips, and she renewed her vow to make change happen, to bring justice for the female half of the human race. I will not give in; I will not stand back and allow this to continue; I will not roll over and allow them to control me and turn me from my resolve to make change happen. I will change things.

Elizabeth felt the surge of power grow in her small, weak body as she made her pledge to the Universe, the women beneath her feet, the women in the world, and those women and girls yet to come. It grew and it grew like a tidal wave until it almost overwhelmed her tiny frame.

It was powerful, and it filled her with a stubborn strength that forged like steel in her heart and mind. That moment it became the mycelia that underpinned her whole life, the very reason for her existence.

She was to remember this powerful moment and draw on its strength for the rest of her life. In moments of despair when she faced the stonewall erected by the patriarchy and in the small hours sat at her writing desk, when she was bone weary but could not spare the time to sleep, she would chant her mantra, justice, justice, justice and receive from the depths of her being, that same surge of power and strength she needed to go on.

Justice, justice, justice!

CHAPTER 5
Independence

The sun was shining, and all nature was newly born that fine May morning. Elizabeth was out walking before breakfast. She couldn't sleep, her head was full of wild thrashing thoughts; plans for the future and fear and trepidation of what her uncle and grandfather would do next: too uneasy for sleep she had risen early and left the house.

She had set her face like flint and refused every overture from them to accept the arranged marriage. George had been incandescent and became violent; slapping her face and threatening to throw her out on the streets. Several confrontations had taken place over the winter, but they had continued to plan the elaborate wedding she told them repeatedly she would never attend.

She had made her own plans. The bottom line was that they were now unwilling to support her as a single woman: neither would provide her with a home and food to eat so she simply must find a way to be independent of them and provide for herself.

This was no easy task, but she hit upon the idea of gaining employment and what better way to meet her needs and give her lots of time for personal study than to become a governess, the perfect answer to her situation. It would take her out of the stranglehold of the family patriarchy; give her independence and a modicum of freedom, whilst allowing her to continue her quest for education and knowledge. Furthermore, it allowed her to hone her skills as a teacher, the thing she wanted to achieve most.

She had applied for several posts without success and as each rejection letter arrived, she grew increasingly desperate. Undaunted, she continued with her applications and had even travelled to several, in-person interviews. What was she doing wrong?

Despite her situation, a sham wedding day looming ahead in July, and the knowledge that beyond that lay disgrace and destitution, she was still resolved never to marry. She would not capitulate; death was preferable to that fate.

Even with all the fear and worry about her present situation, the warm sun on her face, the beautiful white flowers of Spring and the singing of the happy birds lifted her spirits. She walked with a lightness of heart she hadn't felt since Fulneck. I will come through this victorious, she told herself. They will not control my life; I am a free woman and intend to remain so.

As she walked through the fields, she watched the tiny lambs as they gambolled together before rushing back to their mothers, tupping cruelly at their tender, engorged breasts in their selfish quest for milk. She watched as the ewes winced, lifted a leg and flicked their tails with the pain.

Nature is so crude and savage she thought, but that's life I suppose, and we must deal with it as best we can. We must change what we can change and endure, like the dams, that which we cannot.

Returning to her grandfather's house she met the postman on the step. He was delivering a letter, and it was for her. She took it from him and thanked him. Her heart fell when she saw the postmark. She was expecting her usual letter from Harriet or Alice but this bore the mark of Sir Clarence Hermitage! She felt sure it was another rejection.

She had travelled to Manchester the month before for an "in-person" interview at the Midland Hotel and had found Sir Clarence to be a very serious and stern man. She had the feeling that he disapproved of her small stature but there was nothing she could do about that; it was one of the few things she couldn't change so must endure. She had liked the idea of the children though, a girl and a boy and had felt sure that she could teach them well, but she had not allowed herself to hope that she would be successful.

She went to her room and removed her outdoor clothes. Then taking up the letter, she sat at her writing desk and looked at the envelope. She could hardly bear to open it, receiving another rejection would surely deflate her euphoric mood.

Finally, she plucked up the courage to open the missive.

Sir Clarence Hermitage
Hermitage Grange
Bedfordshire

Miss Elizabeth Wolstenholme
12 Lumber Lane
Worsley
Lancashire

12th May 1855

Dear Miss Wolstenholme

I write to confirm your success at our recent meeting and to offer you the position of Governess to my family, here at the Grange. Your employment will commence on 1st June 1855, and your salary will be £50 per annum. The position includes full board and lodgings at the Grange and affords one-week annual holiday leave. It also includes travel with the family as and when appropriate.

I would like to take this opportunity of welcoming you to the Hermitage family and I look forward to you taking up your post as soon as possible.

Yours sincerely

Sir Clarence Hermitage

Elizabeth felt a flood of excitement sweep her body rendering her weak and light-headed. She had to lie down on the bed to stop the room spinning. Here it was, here was her salvation; here was her ticket to independence and her escape from the dreadful marriage they had planned for her.

She was now Miss Elizabeth Wolstenholme, Governess to the Hermitage Family and an independent woman.

She started to laugh, she laughed and laughed; she couldn't stop. She laughed out all the tension, all the fear, all the worry and disappointment of the last months. She laughed till she was limp with the joy of it.

****

George Clarke was in a terrible temper. "Are you insane Elizabeth, no self-respecting man will ever contemplate marriage to you. No man would want to marry a governess. You are consigning yourself to a life of service" he bellowed.

She held her tongue and let him rail, it was not his finest hour, being bested yet again by a woman, and for the second time to boot!

Elizabeth

I am free, I am free, I have done it. They can throw their worse at me now, but they cannot force this ridiculous marriage on me. I am an independent woman, free of the control and influence of the men in my family.

This feels good, so very, very good.

Victory and justice in one fell swoop.

CHAPTER 6
Hermitage Grange

The large Gothic House was exciting but imposing. Having sat her interview in a hotel room in Manchester, this was her first view of it. As the carriage cleared the gates and worked its way up the drive, the sight of it took her breath, and as the horses drew to a halt and the footman opened the doors, Elizabeth had to take a few seconds to gain composure.

The huge front door sported a lion's head knocker in shiny brass, and it was upon this knocker she fixed her eyes to still her beating heart before she climbed from the carriage. The large door slowly opened, and a liveried young man stepped from inside. He was unsmiling and stern and bowing slightly from the waist said "Miss Wolstenholme, I presume?"

She smiled slightly in return and then turned to see her trunk being downloaded.

"I am James the Under Butler," he continued with a cold stare "welcome to Hermitage Grange."

Elizabeth was just about to respond when some loud childish giggling came from the other side of the door and two young children appeared jumping with excitement and jockeying for the best position to see her and to meet her first.

"Hortense and Algernon, I believe." She stepped forward to shake their tiny hands.

Algernon the younger of the two stepped forward with an exaggerated air of importance. "Miss Wolstenholme" he said and taking her hand he shook it firmly.

"And you must be Hortense," said Elizabeth turning to the quiet girl. Hortense stepped forward and curtsied shyly. "Good afternoon, Miss Wolstenholme. May I take you to your room and show you the schoolroom?"

"Indeed, you can, for surely they are the most important rooms in the whole house." She smiled at the children, and they smiled in return.

The children giggled as they took her hand and led her upstairs to a beautiful schoolroom, bright and airy and well-equipped with books and writing materials. A large globe of the world stood on a side table and a large table surrounded by chairs dominated the room. There were noticeboards and a huge blackboard along one wall and one wall was almost completely taken up by windows letting in natural daylight and an amazing view of the gardens and rolling countryside beyond. She stood for a moment and admired the view.

From there the children took her to the next room along the corridor. This was a small tidy room sporting a comfortable chair, a writing desk and a small table. This was her parlour and beyond the parlour her bedroom. This consisted of a large comfortable bed with a colourful patchwork bedspread, a wardrobe and a small chest of drawers. Both of her rooms had an excellent view of the garden and the countryside beyond; she was very pleased. My own little school, she mused.

"Do you like it Miss?" asked Hortense.

"Oh yes, I do indeed. It is very fine and I'm sure I shall be very happy here."

Thus began a happy relationship with the children, but the rest of the staff proved to be more difficult. They didn't see her as one of them, and she certainly wasn't seen as one of the family either; she was expected to exist in a strange no-man's-land, neither one thing nor the other. It was quite disconcerting for Elizabeth as she didn't want to appear aloof, but the downstairs staff were not happy with her joining them for meals or outings.

This was no great hardship for Elizabeth she quickly established a good routine of teaching all morning a light lunch with the children and then on fine days a walk through the park before an evening meal in her little parlour.

The children spent an hour in the early evening with their parents before being bathed and put to bed by their nurse. This gave Elizabeth her evenings for her private study, any writing she wanted to do and any preparation for tomorrow's lessons. She quickly fell into this pattern, and it suited her very well.

Sometime into her post she returned unexpectedly to the school room to retrieve a book and found a young woman apparently reading one of the children's books. The woman was flustered and looked guilty, she had been caught in the act and she was most embarrassed.

"Sorry Miss" she said her face taking on the colour of a newly sliced tomato, "I was just doing the fire."

Elizabeth smiled at her. "No problem; what's your name?"

"Ethel Miss, I'm the scullery maid, I shouldn't really be here." She looked down sheepishly. "I just can't resist popping in when I'm passing. These books are so lovely."

"Would you like to borrow it and read it in your room? I have some superb books I would be more than willing to lend to you."

Ethel's face fell. "That would be lovely Miss, but I can't read, I just look at the pictures."

Elizabeth could have kicked herself, of course the poor girl couldn't read, what was she thinking to embarrass her so? She knew that working-class girls rarely went to school, they were needed at home to tend to younger siblings whilst their mothers went out to work. There was no time for learning and reading in their busy schedules and heavy workloads.

"Would you like me to teach you Ethel, would you like to learn to read?"

The girl's face lit up but then quickly fell again. "The master wouldn't allow it Miss and Mrs Baggot the cook wouldn't like it either. You see she can't read herself and would think I was trying to get one up on her. Besides I'm just a girl and my dad says girls have much smaller brains than boys so can't learn things easily."

Elizabeth stared at her. "Girls are just as capable as boys Ethel, despite what your father says and neither the master nor Mrs Baggot can stop you learning to read if you really want to. As long as you are doing it in your own time; they have no right to stop you. What time do you usually retire to bed?"

"8:00 pm Miss"

"Then, if you come to the schoolroom at 7:00 pm, we can spend one hour on your reading lesson. We could start tonight. How does, that sound?"

Ethel looked excited. "I cannot pay you Miss I have no money of my own. I send it all home to my parents for the family pot."

"Who said anything about money? Here Ethel, take this book to your room and look at the pictures as often as you like. You will soon be reading the works of Charles Dickens I promise you."

Elizabeth looked pensive she was skating on thin ice, and she knew it. If this got out among the other staff, it would soon come to the attention of Sir Clarence who might not take too kindly to his servants learning to read. She must tell him herself what she is doing then everything would be above board; honesty was always the best policy.

Later that day when the children went off with their nurse, she gently tapped on Sir Clarence's office door. There was no answer, he obviously wasn't in there and she turned to go but then, there he was just coming down the main stairs dressed for dinner. He stopped when he saw her and where she was positioned.

"Miss Wolstenholme" he asked with a question in his voice.

"Sir Clarence, I was wondering if you could spare me two short minutes of your time?"

"Of course, but I must tell you that I don't usually have anything to do with household matters. I leave that to my dear wife, Lady Constance."

"I appreciate that sir, but this particular matter does need your attention."

Sir Clarence nodded and passing her he opened the office door and then stepped back to allow her to enter ahead of him. "Two minutes then."

"Sir Clarence, there is a young woman at work in your kitchens. She is very bright and eager to learn to read. I have offered to teach her, in her own time and in my own time. I am asking your permission as she is afraid that you would not be pleased with her for doing so. I assured her that I would make sure that you knew what we were going to do and that you approved of her desire to read. Do you give me permission to teach this young woman please?"

Sir Clarence was taken aback. She saw the struggle going on in his mind. He walked over to his desk and sat in the chair. "Miss Wolstenholme, I'm not sure that this is the best course of action. She is of lowly station, how can books and reading be of any benefit to her? Surely as a woman, she will have no time for reading, she will marry soon and have many children; your labours will be wasted."

Elizabeth could feel the anger rising but she was well-practiced at controlling it. "But Sir Clarence, forgive me but can't you see that what you have just said is so very unfair and wrong? Look at your own children, would you be happy if Hortense could not read but Algernon could? Surely you can see that if you teach someone to read you open up a whole new world of learning. You and I could transform this young woman's life. I am willing to give as many hours as possible to give her that chance."

Sir Clarence stared at her and luckily, he wasn't an unreasonable man he had just simply never thought about such things before. He fell back onto his usual pomposity and replied. "If you want to waste your time and efforts on such things, I cannot really stop you. I perceive that you are so passionate about it that you will find a way of doing it anyway."

He fell silent for a few seconds and then smiled. "Thank you for telling me, I appreciate that you haven't gone behind my back" and with that, he walked from the room.

***

At 7:00 pm that night Ethel arrived in the school room where Elizabeth was waiting for her.

"Come in Ethel and welcome to my schoolroom; please sit down. First things first, I want you to know that you need not be afraid of anyone stopping you from learning to read or disagreeing with your lessons. I have spoken to Sir Clarence, and he has approved my teaching you to read, just as long as we do it in our own time. So, from now on it is lesson time at this time every night, except Sunday when I think we both deserve a night off."

Ethel's face was a picture, she turned quite red, and tears filled her eyes. She expressed gratitude to Elizabeth and Elizabeth in return told her that she must grasp the chance offered and work hard.

Ethel proved to be a good scholar learning eagerly and really quickly. She was soon reading the early reader books that were in the school room and things were going really well but then; Mrs Baggot the cook found out.

They were about a month into their lessons when on a wet and windy Wednesday Ethel failed to arrive for her lesson. Elizabeth waited but by 8:00 pm it was obvious that Ethel was not going to come, so Elizabeth went in search of her.

Going below stairs she could hear the mumbling of the staff around the fire in their common room. She moved on to the kitchen area and that was where she found Ethel. She was sat in the hearth cleaning the fire dogs. She was filthy black from the black lead and covered in rust that her wire wool had dislodged from the filthy grating where the coals sat.

"Ethel, what's this? Why this sort of work at this time of night?"

"Oh Miss, Cook has given me this job to do every night from now on. She found me reading the back of a bag of rice and realised I have been learning to read. She questioned me closely and I couldn't lie, I had to tell her about my lessons. She was very angry."

At this, Ethel began to sob her tears trickling through the black dust on her face leaving streaks of white in the black.

Elizabeth turned and walked towards the servants' common room, pulling back her shoulders and lifting her head as high as she could she stepped into the room theatrically. All conversation stopped abruptly, and every eye turned to look at her.

"Why is my pupil still working at this time of night?" she asked.

Mr Collins the butler replied. "It's up to Cook when her scullery-maid works not the governess."

Cook sniffed and nodded her head but did not speak.

"Forgive me Mr Collins but Ethel has a contract for so many hours a day and that contract cannot be changed at the whim of another employee. I put it to you that Ethel is being denied her reading lesson because it does not suit you or Mrs Baggot that she gets an education. I suggest that you revert to her usual, contracted hours with immediate effect."

Mr Collins stood to attention. "It is of little consequence what you think Miss, I shall be going to the Master first thing to get this nonsense stopped."

Elizabeth smiled. "Oh, I should like to see that Mr Collins as Sir Clarence has given me full permission to teach Ethel at our convenience, just so long as we do it in our own time. So, let me make myself abundantly clear, you will cease your persecution of this young woman forthwith or I shall be passing on my complaint to Sir Clarence."

There was a deathly silence and Elizabeth slowly turned to walk out of the room, but she was stopped in her tracks by a woman's voice.

"Miss Wolstenholme, may I join the class too, please? I was never allowed to go to school, there were eight of us you see, and I was needed at home. Can I learn to read too? I won't be any trouble."

She turned to see an anxious-faced young woman, slightly older than Ethel, but her face was as eager and her eyes bright. Elizabeth knew that it had taken a lot for this young woman to speak out in front of Collins and Baggot.

"What's your name?"

"Betty Miss."

"Well Betty, 7:00 pm in the schoolroom, we'll start tomorrow." Then turning to the room at large, she continued "If there's anyone else that wants to learn, all are welcome in my schoolroom from 7:00 pm onwards, do not be shy or afraid, just come along."

With that, Elizabeth walked from the room and up the stairs.

****

What pleasant days those were in Hermitage Grange. The children were a delight to teach, and she enjoyed telling them stories about the fierce lion on the front door. How his job was to guard the house but really, he was a bit of a coward. He was frightened of the world and all that was in it. He had to learn how to be brave and bold.

The children decided his name was Lionel and he became their favourite character. He kept them safe when nightmares came and was there to welcome them back every time they returned to the house.

The staff lessons went from strength to strength. On the first night she had four pupils, but the number quickly grew until there was only Mrs Baggot the Cook and Mr Collins the Butler who didn't attend. Mrs Baggot because she was too proud to admit she couldn't read and Mr Collins because he claimed he could read already. Elizabeth suspected that he could read well enough to keep the ledgers, but he wasn't really competent enough to read a book.

Within her first year she taught 12 members of staff to read, and they were devouring the books in the schoolroom. It was time to take the matter to Sir Clarence again.

"Miss Wolstenholme, I hear that I have to thank you for Lionel the Lion?" He had a large smile across his face which Elizabeth returned.

"I cannot tell a lie, he was one of the first things I saw on my arrival at Hermitage Grange, he has such character, he sort of evolved into the kindly lion who keeps us all safe."

They were talking about a series of stories Elizabeth had written to entertain the children and encourage them to make up their own tales of Lionel the Lion. She had not realised that the children had taken the stories to their father.

"Well, he has certainly established himself in my children's lives. Thank you, Miss Wolstenholme. Now you want to see me on another matter I believe?"

"Yes Sir, it's the lessons I have been teaching to the staff. I now have half a dozen competent readers who have read every book in the nursery at least once and have also read my Dickens Collection. I am very proud of them; they have worked so hard and are deriving such pleasure from reading."

"Bravo, well done, I must say I am very surprised that the women have been capable of learning as well as the men."

Elizabeth drew in her breath and swallowed the disgust that rose in her throat. "I need to offer them more reading material. I was wondering if I could borrow a few suitable books from your library?"

"Of course, of course, I should have thought of it myself. Feel free to use the library anytime you like although I must admit, some of the tomes in there haven't been read for many years."

He chuckled then went on "I too have been thinking about your lessons for the staff, how about we throw your talents open to the people that work outside the house? A Sunday School of some sort?"

She was taken aback. "Why Yes of course! What a lovely idea."

Elizabeth

This teaching business is even more fulfilling than I supposed. The children are wonderful, and the staff members are so keen to learn. There is only Baggot and Collins who are doggedly opposed to everything I do. There are times when I suspect that my food is not up to the same standard as that of the other staff members, but I know that Ethel and Betty keep a close eye on Mrs Baggott, so I am confident they will not allow her to poison me!

Mr Collins is icily cold towards me and somehow sees me as some sort of enemy. I don't understand people like them; happy with the status quo and opposed to any change. Happy to remain the doormats of these titled families and eat the crumbs thrown from their table. But I must not voice such opinions, were they to find out about my activities in

Manchester with the Socialists and the Secularists, they would surely get me sacked and thrown out.

A worrying letter from Grandfather today; he doesn't sound his usual self. Tells me he is ill and asks me to forgive him for allowing George to treat me so badly. Says I should have been allowed to go to Bedford College: too late now Grandfather. Reading between the lines I fear there is trouble brewing. However, I still have a few short months left here at Hermitage Grange, Hortense and Algernon are off to boarding school in September and my work for the family will be complete.

Two children all educated in preparation to move on, Algernon will do well at Harrow, but I fear for Hortense; the school she is going to does not offer a good curriculum. I pointed this out to Sir Clarence who said it was the best of a bad bunch and I had to agree. The state of girls' education is dire, and I would be ashamed to send a daughter of mine to such a place. I should have been bold and suggested he allowed me to stay on and teach her myself; I could have made a much better job of it. I did of course suggest Fulneck, but Sir Clarence said it was too far from Hermitage Grange. That I did my best is all I can console myself with.

I will correspond with her as she charts her course through the minefield of boarding school; I can at least encourage her and remind her that Lionel the Lion will always be protecting her.

In my 3 years at Hermitage Grange, I have taught 30 members of staff to read and write and I leave this place with a feeling of achievement. 19 women now read and write, and I have promised to correspond with each and every one of them.

CHAPTER 7
Roe Green Again

Another funeral; this time it's grandfather. She had received his letter some six weeks ago. He had opened his heart and in shaky handwriting, told her he wasn't much longer for this world and begged her forgiveness. She had of course written back forgiving him completely and telling him that coming to Hermitage Grange had been the very best thing that could have happened to her.

She had said that the children of the family were bright and respectful and teaching them had been a joy. She told him about the two young servants Ethel and Betty and how all the others had wanted lessons and that she had taught them all to read in the evenings and at her Sunday School: it was very satisfying being a teacher. She explained that the children were now ready to leave home for boarding school and she asked if she could return to his house until she decided what her next career move would be, and he had responded with delight but asked her to hurry as he could feel his strength ebbing by the day and feared his life was nearing its conclusion.

She had asked Sir Clarence if she could terminate her employment two weeks early in order to reach her grandfather and he had agreed and paid her an extra amount as a special thank-you for all the extra work she had done. However, pneumonia, the old man's friend, had stepped in and her grandfather died before she made it back to Roe Green.

She was here now, the funeral behind her, looking once again at Uncle George but this time he had no power over her. She had reached her majority; she was a successful woman with money and position. He would not make eye contact, but she had no worries about that, for she was the victor, and she knew what male pride looked like; unlike him, she bore no grudge and looked upon her childhood as her "first piece of martyrdom" to the cause of justice for women.

They were sat around the desk in grandfather's study where his solicitor was sitting with Richard Clarke's will open before him. He began to read. The bulk of the estate was being left to her grandmother for the duration of her lifetime but upon her death, it was to go to Joseph. No surprise there then.

She closed off what the man was saying as he began rhyming off the small gifts her grandfather was bestowing on faithful servants and his charitable causes. At least grandmother was being looked after and the house was staying in the family. She wondered if Joseph would move in and look after his grandmother: she doubted it, he had made a fine life for himself as a teacher of mathematics at Cambridge University; he would not want to come back north.

Her attention was suddenly grabbed by the man speaking her name. She reeled in shock! Grandfather had left her £3,000; she could hardly breathe. Uncle George looked shocked and angry, Joseph and her grandmother looked delighted. Elizabeth had lost all colour from her face; she was glad she was sitting as otherwise she may well have fallen down. The solicitor wrapped up the proceedings and left.

Well, well, well you did redeem yourself Grandfather, thought Elizabeth as she sat in the drawing room with her tea before her. She was without words, and that was a very rare thing indeed. This is going to make all the difference to my life and work. She allowed the thought to sink in whilst taking several deep breaths.

Her grandmother spoke "I'm so pleased for you Elizabeth, your grandfather and I discussed his will just before he died, it is something he really wanted to do. Make sure you were provided for in case your plans went awry. Any idea what you will do with your inheritance?"

George and Joseph looked at her in expectation.

Elizabeth didn't need to think now. "I shall open a girls' school, I will provide a first-class, education for girls, I will try to make a difference, give them the chance I was denied."

"Bravo!" said Joseph.

"Well done," said her grandmother but George Wolstenholme was silent.

Elizabeth
Well, well, well, what a surprise, life is full of new beginnings. When one door closes another one opens, as they say. I thought I would be looking for new employment, another rich family whose children needed a

governess, and now here I am looking for premises to open my own school and begin my campaign to improve education for girls everywhere.

I didn't think for one minute that Grandpa would leave me an inheritance, but he has and a fine one too. I have found a building just up the road in Boothstown and I now have the money to be up and running for the new school year. Sir Clarence Hermitage has given me an excellent reference so I can begin advertising places. I have persuaded my stepmother Mary to be housekeeper so that is in amazingly good hands.

I am so grateful for my time at Hermitage Grange and in thanks to Sir Clarence and Lady Constance, I intend to call my school The Grange School for Girls.

Thanks be to the Universe.

CHAPTER 8
The Grange School
Boothstown

Seven years later the Grange School, Boothstown had grown in popularity and was a roaring success. Her school offered a full and comprehensive curriculum for young girls and one of her first pupils was Hortense Hermitage which was an amazing endorsement and gave the school a high profile from its inception.

Elizabeth was drawing on her experiences teaching the staff at Hermitage Grange and her girls were happy and taught to think independently and question all things. She would often chuckle to herself when she remembered one of her father's clergymen friends who had described her as "a natural sceptic who questioned everything;" what a perfect description and she was passing it on.

Not bad, she thought, a good outcome for my years of work. A school at full capacity and a waiting list of pupils. My curriculum has been enthusiastically received and the girls are benefiting from the Wolstenholme touch. Now here I stand at some 28 years of age, headmistress of a successful school and a member of the College of Preceptors.

With the Preceptors she had been taking an interest in the proposed Education Bill and she was regularly writing to MPs to convey her dislike of the Bill and the necessity for it to include girls and not just boys. She had learned of the Taunton Commission, set up by Parliament to look at the Bill before it went into the House to be debated and voted on. She had written and asked to speak at it and put forward her case.

"Don't be ridiculous Elizabeth! No woman has ever spoken before a Parliamentary Commission before, you will never be allowed to do so" said her old friend and ally Harriet.

"You mean no woman has, until now: nothing ventured, nothing gained." She smiled at her friend in an uncharacteristic manner. Harriet chuckled knowing that her friend needed no encouragement to take on the patriarchy.

Elizabeth knew that her work was paying off and that she was being taken seriously so she was very pleased, but not very surprised when her invitation came in the post, and she travelled to London to be the first woman ever to speak before a parliamentary commission.

Travelling down to London on the train with Harriet beside her, she was nervous and more than a little afraid. She was continually swamped with a feeling of being outside her abilities and not up to the task. The brief conversation with Harriet in the parlour had been more bravado and theatre than fearlessness and bravery but in no way would she ever back out of this situation.

When their cab arrived, she looked through the window at the great Palace of Westminster and her courage failed her. Alighting onto the pavement her legs were like jelly. She closed her eyes and swayed slightly and then suddenly she reached out and grasped Harriet's hand.

Harriet was taken aback; this was new, she thought. Elizabeth was usually so self-confident and self-assured. She stood for a moment pondering what to do.

"Elizabeth' she said eventually, "look at me."   Elizabeth opened her eyes. "The women and girls of this country need you. There is no one willing or able to stand up and fight for them. They need justice Elizabeth, and you are the only one in the position to speak for them. Now come on show some backbone and stop being silly."

She was staring earnestly at Elizabeth the whole time. Elizabeth pulled her eyes away and closing them she listened to the words in her head. Justice, justice, justice and, opening her eyes, she took a deep breath and stepped forward towards the great Palace of Westminster for the first time, a ground-breaking moment for the women of England and little did she know that this place was to feature massively in her life and that she was to become known to every MP as the "Scourge of the Commons."

However, on this day she cut a very tiny but authoritative figure standing before those great men. She gained strength from her mantra and gave the speech of her life thus far.

"One of the many things I am so distressed about is the total paucity of girls' education in this country. What little there is available, is of poor quality and very limited. Girls should receive the same education as boys to enhance their lives and equip them for a life of independence both emotionally and financially; only through education can a woman be truly free."

She made an impression, she was listened to and as a result, the Taunton Commission advised that the proposed Bill be changed to include girls as well as boys and the following year the Act was passed into Law. All children, regardless of gender, received a state education from the age of 5 till 13 years.

This was Elizabeth Wolstenholme's first little piece of justice.

Elizabeth

What an amazing day I've had. Who would have thought that I, Elizabeth Wolstenholme, would be the first woman to speak before a parliamentary commission? However, I must not let such things go to my head, there is a job to be done and until women have the vote and female MPs are present in the House, I cannot and will not rest.

Onwards and upwards

. Justice, justice, justice.

CHAPTER 9
Contagious Diseases

"I can't believe it." Elizabeth is reading a report from her friend Josephine Butler. "This simply cannot be true. To think that this is happening, and it is sanctioned by law: this must stop."

She is staring wide-eyed across the desk at Mary who, true to form, is looking bemused. Elizabeth often did this; read something and then talked to Mary as though Mary had read it with her and could hear her thought process. It always left Mary confused and worried about what was coming next.

"You're doing it again dear, I'm not a party to your thoughts; you need to explain."

Elizabeth closed her eyes and shook her head. "Of course; sorry Mother. This is one of a number of reports sent to me by Mrs Butler; the treatment of women and girls under this abomination called the Contagious Diseases Act. The Government is worried about venereal disease; it's spreading like wildfire in garrison towns and ports. Aldershot in particular has a staggering 50% of its soldiers infected. Of course, according to the male doctors and our learned male MPs, it's not their fault. No, apparently men don't pass these diseases on they are only passed on from female to male and never the other way round: though how the women get it in the first place and how the disease knows the difference is not explained. No, apparently it's all the fault of these poor working-class women in such a place of despair that they are forced to sell their bodies to feed themselves and their children.

Worse than that the police have been given carte blanche to arrest any woman who they think may be a prostitute. I am just reading some of the appalling stories about what befalls these unfortunate women when they fall into the hands of the authorities. Forcibly examined for signs of disease, using torturous instruments. Six men in attendance!! Disgusting, this is state-sanctioned sexual assault."

Mary's colour had drained from her face. She reached out a hand and took the report that Elizabeth was offering to her. She sat back and read it. After some time, she looked up from her deliberations and with a facial expression that reflected her horror she said. "Elizabeth, I cannot believe what I am reading. Innocent women, not just prostitutes."

"Mother, they are all innocent! These women who sell their bodies are not doing it by choice but out of necessity! They are trying to feed themselves and their children in most cases. Do not judge them by your own "Christian" standards. They are the victims of male oppression: no, we will fight this battle and we will win without making any distinction between the women. They are all victims, all of them, every last one."

Mary looked at Elizabeth's earnest face and then nodded. "Yes, dearest you are right as ever, they are all victims of this cruel, unfair law. I take it you are joining this campaign?"

"It's hardly a campaign as yet, but if I can persuade Mrs Butler to put her name to it, it will give it respectability. I cannot move without having the wrath of the God-fearing establishment fall upon me personally if I make a stand and speak out publicly on this topic. You know what it's like for single women; we are supposed to be pure as the driven snow and totally unaware of such things; the usual double standards. I cannot write or speak about anything on this topic as I am supposed to have no knowledge of sexual congress – ridiculous!"

"Yes dear" Mary blushed and looked away.

Elizabeth sighed and returned to her postbag. Elizabeth's attention was fixed on the plight of one particular young girl Nancy Martin. Daughter of a poor washerwoman in Aldershot, she had been helping her mother by returning some freshly laundered clothes to some soldiers at the garrison. She was just 13 years old, but a policeman stopped her and searched through her pockets where he found a shilling piece. She explained that it was payment for the laundry, but he chose not to believe her.

She was arrested and taken to the police cells where she was forcibly examined by the police doctor in the presence of a further five policemen. She was restrained by straps to a metal table and the doctor used instruments to carry out an intimate examination which was so painful that Nancy screamed and writhed throwing her body this way and that trying to stop the torture; the poor child injured her back on the metal edge of the table. The whole examination should have taken around three minutes, but Nancy's ordeal lasted for over 45. Finally, the doctor admitted that Nancy was clean, and Nancy was released to drag herself home, bleeding and in terrible pain.

At first, her mother thought the child had been set upon and sexually abused on her way home from her errand but when she ascertained the full details from her distraught child, she realised she had no protection. In fact, she knew that any young girl who had been interfered with like this would be considered easy game for any of the many soldiers that inhabited the town. She feared that Nancy would be attacked again and feared for the girl's future.

When Elizabeth read the details of the case, she knew she had to act. She wrote to the mother assuring her that she was working on Nancy's behalf. She then wrote to Josephine Butler drawing her attention to the need to help this poor girl and Josephine used her influence in society to contact Lady Marchmount, an ally in the cause, who offered Nancy a place as Lady's Maid to her young daughter. Thus, Nancy was dispatched out of Aldershot and its dangers into the peace and quiet of the English Countryside.

So many cases came over Elizabeth's desk, great postbags full to brimming; so many horrible stories, that she realised that this Act of Parliament, this so-called law, simply gave men the freedom to sexually abuse women, and women had no protection at all.

Elizabeth

I simply must do something about this. Mrs Butler works with working-class women and prostitutes; she has written papers, very knowledgeable papers at that, the woman is an inspiration. What Josephine Butler doesn't know about this topic isn't worth knowing at all. If I can persuade her to work with me on this campaign, if I can get her to use her name and influence to head it up, then we could move towards getting a repeal of this atrocious act and justice for women and girls everywhere.

Men force women to adhere to a much higher moral code than they themselves practice, this act is a piece of absolute hypocrisy. This Act is misogyny of the basest kind and the cruellest kind of class legislation, so very unjust and so very, very wrong. With Mrs Butler's name giving me protection, I can make this happen.

Justice, justice, justice.

****

"Mother, I have been asked to address a meeting in the Free Trade Hall! It is mostly men, and the topic is the Contagious Diseases Act. The organisers have read my letters and articles for the Manchester Guardian and know of the petition I have set up. Apparently, this group of working men can be quite difficult and have been known to harangue speakers, even going as far as to throw tomatoes! This feels like it is going to be a challenge."

"Just say no Elizabeth, if it's too intimidating, just refuse. Let them get a man to do it. Just say no." Mary sounded exasperated; she was worried for Elizabeth's safety.

"Oh no mother, it has to be me. I am the most knowledgeable one on the subject and this group of men need to be on our side. Have no fear Mother, I can win them over. It won't be easy, but I am up to the job."

****

The hall was filled to capacity and humming with expectation. Elizabeth was standing in the wings peeping out trying to ascertain the atmosphere of the room, trying to get a feeling for the mood of the men in the rows of seats. She was nervous. Her legs felt weak and shaky, and she trembled slightly as she prepared to go out onto the podium. She had spoken many, many times to large gatherings such as this. She had addressed men-only crowds from a public platform, but this time was quite different. The topic was viewed as contentious, and she was a single woman, who should not be speaking about such things. The men she was addressing were not the educated, middle-class types she was used to talking to, these were rough, working-class men from the local mills and factories. Her palms were moist, and she could feel the sweat running between her shoulder blades as she walked out to address the crowd.

There were the expected cheers and whistles as she stood, but then seeing how small she was, they fell silent. Elizabeth waited until she had complete silence and then spoke:

"Men of Manchester. I perceive that you are decent, clean-living men and I appeal to your sense of fairness and decency. Have you a wife? A daughter? Maybe you have a loving sister? I know that every last one of you has a mother. How would you feel if that loved one was arrested whilst walking home? Not just arrested but forcibly and painfully examined by untrained men, who were actually enjoying the situation?

Yes, yes you would be very angry and you would want to avenge and protect her, but you cannot because this law gives the police complete freedom to carry out these dreadful procedures and if they decide your sister, wife, mother, is carrying a disease they will imprison her in a "Lock Hospital" and continue these examinations until such time they consider her clean."

Silence had fallen, the rowdy comments had ceased: she had their full attention. She told them Nancy's story; they were shocked and angry. By the time she had finished speaking, the men clapped reverently and then queued to sign her petition.

"A good night's work Elizabeth. What a bricky girl you are." There was pride and admiration in Mary's voice.

Elizabeth

I meet with women and the stories I hear are the stuff of nightmares. I have certainly completed my education on the plight of working-class women and their total dependency on men. It seems that their one and only goal in life is to marry but it affords them no freedom of autonomy and they are destined to be slaves to their own bodily functions.

What a sad fact of life and it is so unnecessary. If women and men had true equality, then women would be educated and able to enter professions and earn their own money. Instead, what we have is women being totally owned and used by men. Working-class men often work hard to keep their families fed but still use their women as chattels and expect their subservience.

Sometimes they grow tired of the situation and take to drink, which further exacerbates the plight of the women. They are often driven into extreme poverty and left alone when their feckless husbands abandon them. Left with the dilemma of hungry mouths to feed and no possibility of work they take to the oldest profession and again it is men who call the shots. It is all so utterly depressing, and the law of the land blames these poor women for their state and affords them no protection.

Josephine at least is as ardent an advocate for these poor women as I am. They have no one to champion their cause, we must stand together and highlight their plight; they are the victims of society and men in particular.

It would be so easy to hate men, every last one of them, but there are good men out there, good men and true, and some are working with us to bring about the end of this vile Act. John Stuart Mill for instance, exemplary in every way, and Mr William T Stead, dedicated and hard-working for the cause of female emancipation, fine men both.

The Contagious Diseases Act is indeed the most horrendous piece of legislation, discriminatory and very wrong; but it is not the only one. The whole of English Law discriminates against women and girls, seeing them as it does as second-class citizens: it is a fact that some farm animals have more rights than young women. The fact that under the law of the land, married women are unable to have their own finances or keep their own property upon marriage is a total disgrace and opens them to abuse of all kinds.

The Law is an ass and needs to change.

Justice, justice, justice.

Josephine Butler and Elizabeth began a work that was to take the best part of 20 years to bear fruit. They worked long and hard speaking, writing pamphlets and gathering names on petitions against this cruel, discriminatory act.

The Elizabeth Burley case in 1881, where an innocent 18-year-old girl was chased through the streets of Dover and threw herself into the dock to escape the pursuing Policemen, was the catalyst that finally brought about the repeal of this terrible act, but not until 1886.

CHAPTER 10
Free Love

"Free love? As if love is anything but free! Man has bought brains, but all the millions in the world have failed to buy love. Man has subdued bodies, but all the power on earth has been unable to subdue love. Man has conquered whole nations, but all his armies could not conquer love. Man has chained and fettered the spirit, but he has been utterly helpless before love. High on a throne, with all the splendour and pomp his gold can command, man is yet poor and desolate, if love passes him by. And if it stays, the poorest hovel is radiant with warmth, with life and colour. Thus, love has the magic power to make of a beggar a king. Yes, love is free; it can dwell in no other atmosphere."
Emma Goldman

"You always have your nose in a book Elizabeth, what is it this time? It must be good you haven't put it down since you received it two days ago." Mary was looking quizzically across the tea table. There was a fondness between the two, a true mother-and-daughter relationship had grown between them over the years and now Elizabeth could not be without Mary for very long and needed her steadiness and unconditional love. To Mary, Elizabeth was the child she had never had, and she was devoted to her. Looking up sheepishly Elizabeth responded shyly.

"I don't know if I even dare to tell you Mother, I fear you will be very shocked." Pausing slightly, she continued "I have discussed with you before how Mary Wollstonecraft and others chose to live with their partners rather than marry and become the property of their husbands, well it seems the idea is spreading. There is a movement called the Free Love Movement which advocates a Free Union, and a number of prominent women are choosing this course: I must say that I find it all rather exciting."

Mary looked alarmed "Oh dear, you are not thinking of embarking upon such a reckless course of action, are you Elizabeth?"

Elizabeth smiled kindly at her. "Not at the moment Mother, there is no man in my life with whom I would want to live and share my earthly possessions, but I cannot help admiring these women and would support them if I'm called upon to do so, stand with them and share their conviction. They are pushing the boundaries, and the boundaries need pushing. There are some pretty impressive names on the list; I think I will attend the next lecture."

"Be careful Elizabeth, look out for your reputation, you are a respected and successful teacher and businesswoman. Don't throw it away on some hair-brained campaign that is doomed to failure."

Elizabeth smiled indulgently at Mary. "I have shared with you before that I consider marriage, as it stands in English Law, to be no different than enslavement or prostitution. Things have to change, and they will only change if we make them change. Justice Mother justice."

With that, Elizabeth returned to her book. Mary sighed and began to gather up the tea dishes she knew full well that Elizabeth could not be dissuaded from her quest for justice and had learned long ago that Elizabeth would dig in her heels if she pursued the matter further. Better to just let her get on with it, she usually knew what she was doing.

A week later found Elizabeth in a packed hall in central Manchester. The audience, mostly young women, contained some angry men as well. The speakers were Annie Besant and Charles Bradlaugh people that she knew all about, having read their work.

Bradlaugh and Besant were prominent Secularists and were living in a "Free Union." Annie had shocked society with a public divorce citing her husband as an abuser and had fought a hard-won court case to prove the matter. Charles was a leading free-thinker and gifted public speaker. Both had many enemies in the establishment particularly the church, who felt that they were threatening public decency by aiming to change society for the betterment of women.

She listened enraptured to their lecture and heard Annie call for a different kind of sexual morality. One where men and women could freely choose to commit to each other because of the love they felt and not out of legal or economic necessity.

She listened intently as Charles spoke of voluntary motherhood, where a woman has the right to say no to her husband. Her body is her own and she should have the choice if and when to have children. No woman should ever be a slave to her own fertility and have to endure enforced maternity.

The lecture was a watershed for Elizabeth. This is everything she wanted to hear and right before her eyes stood two people who were living out their convictions in the full public gaze. When the lecture concluded Charles and Annie stood together on stage and the women gave thunderous applause. A few of the men tried to boo and shout them down but they were outnumbered. Charles and Annie left the stage, the crowd began to disperse and still Elizabeth sat, deep in her thoughts with Annie's words ringing in her ears.

"My judges preach against free love openly, yet they practice it secretly."

That night she became a committed member of the Free Love Movement.

Elizabeth

I could hardly believe my ears! Here were two people, "living in sin" according to the church, openly talking in straightforward language, about the hows and whys of the situation. Marriage is just prostitution or slavery for women; women are slaves to their own fertility. Why are men allowed to pursue their sexual instincts whilst women are supposed to consider the sex act as something they dislike, whilst men are expected to "sow their wild oats" and follow any animalistic instinct they desire?

Annie says, "they say one thing, whilst doing another!"

I shall never marry but if I met a man that I could love and respect, a man who showed me love and respect, then I may well consider a Free Union. It certainly works well for Annie and Charles; they are both happy and fulfilled.

Cheese and crusts! What silly thoughts I am having, I shall never be able to have a Free Union, how can a respectable teacher like myself even contemplate such a thing? No, it would be the end of my days as a teacher, the parents would never tolerate a headmistress who lived as they say, "over the brush."

PART TWO

Branching Out
1867 - 1890

CHAPTER 11
Time for Change

"We need bigger premises" she announced at dinner on a cold bleak December evening just before Christmas. We have more girls wanting to enrol than we have places to fill, we must expand to accommodate them.

"That's a huge step Elizabeth" said Joseph her brother, who was up for the Christmas Holiday.

"Indeed, it is Joseph, but I have thought about it and in order to expand my curriculum and influence more girls, it is the next logical step." She paused for effect then continued. "I have been making enquires and I think I have found the ideal place. Congleton in Cheshire, a building called Moody Hall. A large building with outbuildings for extra classrooms and in the middle of the most glorious countryside; so reminiscent of Fulneck, I fell in love with it straight away. I have quite set my mind; we will move there in the New Year."

"So, you have done the deed? You have signed?" Joseph responded in astonishment.

"No, not quite, but I intend to at the earliest convenience, I have a verbal agreement; I am quite resolved."

"Well Elizabeth I cannot but concede to your greater knowledge and intellect; you rarely make mistakes, but I cannot see the logic of moving from a City like Manchester, with your network of allies and. backers, to the middle of the Cheshire countryside. All your contacts are here, all the influential things you are involved with are based here in Manchester. Why would you take yourself off to the middle of nowhere?

"Joseph, ye of little faith! Have you never heard of the railway? Congleton is not that remote and has a railway station. The place is perfect for the girls and the building is a very fine, well-appointed Georgian house in the town centre and the railway station is less than a mile away.

Manchester air is not the best for growing girls; the beautiful countryside around Fulneck was one of the many things that made the school so delightful to me. Learning is much more enjoyable in natural surroundings."

She was excited and undaunted by such a huge step and moved forward into the Spring of 1867 with a light heart and a resolve to make her school the greatest girls' school in the land.

****

"Mother, are you happy to move with me? I know you are not getting any younger, but you seem still to be strong and able. I will be sad if you feel that you are ready for a well-earned retirement but will fully understand. I can assure you that I have no desire to work you into the ground. Please be honest."

Mary Wolstenholme looked up from her sewing. She never failed to be surprised by her stepdaughter's straight-talking. She never held back, never kept anything to herself.

"Elizabeth dearest, where would I go if not with you?"

"I was thinking that if it came to it and we had to part company, you might want to consider a rest home on the coast. I am sure that I could stretch our coffers to accommodate such a move if it was your desire. I owe you so much it is the least I can do to make sure that your old age is honoured and catered for. I love you as I would have my own mother had she lived, and you have certainly treated me as such in return."

Mary's face broke into a smile and tears filled her eyes. "Elizabeth, that is the most endearing thing I have ever heard but can I too be honest?"

Elizabeth nodded her assent and Mary continued "Even if I was feeling incapable of work, which I most definitely am not, then I would want to stay by your side, be with you in my dotage. To be apart from you would be the cruellest thing I can imagine."

Elizabeth looked at her intently and replied, "Then that is what will happen, and I promise you that I will stick to my part of the bargain no matter what" and with that she rose from her seat and joining her mother on the settee they hugged warmly.

"Now we must plan properly, for you will not be able to run such a large establishment single-handed. We will need a housemaid and a kitchen maid so we must put up the advertisements along with those for extra teaching staff; onwards and upwards, let's think this thing through."

So the plans were laid, and all things put into place for their move from Boothstown, on the outskirts of Manchester, to Congleton, and it was in May 1867 Elizabeth Wolstenholme moved her school to Moody Hall, Moody Street, Congleton in Cheshire.

****

Congleton was a small mill town set in the rolling Cheshire countryside. Set in a valley it had a thriving market and a huge fairground. It was an old town steeped in history but had a rather closed, narrow-minded community. However, it also had a thriving Cooperative movement with lecture rooms and a programme of education for the mill workers along the same lines as the Mechanics Institute she knew so well.

Much to her dismay she also found that the church had a very firm grip on the town, and it was not to her liking at all, but she also quickly established that there was a small band of Secularists already at work.

All this information was derived from friends in the Preceptors and Secularist movement in Manchester and one name that was mentioned frequently was, Benjamin John Elmy. She was advised to find Ben Elmy and get working with him on the education of his workers, particularly the women. She was told that Ben wanted to extend the educational programme and that he was an ardent feminist, actively fighting for the vote and proud to say so.

CHAPTER 12
Benjamin John Elmy

Thursday evening 11:00 pm, Benjamin John Elmy stands in his cutting room surveying all he owns. The end of a busy week meant it was payday tomorrow. He was looking forward to it in anticipation and a sort of triumphant excitement.

His Fustian cutters were all women, and he knew "they" would be appearing tomorrow at the mill gate, the husbands, the fathers, the sons and even some brothers. They'd be tripping up Havannah Street to the mill office to collect the earnings of his hard-working women; he would be waiting for them. No man was getting the money due to his women; if they wanted an Elmy wage packet, they must earn it themselves. He had been doing this for months now but still they came, still they argued and pressed him saying it was the Law of the Land, and still he stood steadfast and resolute before their onslaught.

An ardent feminist and radical fighter for the cause of female emancipation, he was taking this stand, and it was well-planned. He would give a speech and tell them yet again in no uncertain words, that women who work for Ben Elmy would be given their money in their hand, as was their due and their right. No Elmy money would be given to husbands, fathers, sons or brothers: the women had earned the money, and it was theirs to do with as they saw fit.

He knew he had made enemies, and not just among the fathers and husbands, but among the mill owners too, but he was resolute, you can't make an omelette without breaking eggs as the saying goes. He had put his hand to the plough a long time ago, he was well acquainted with "the struggle" and he would not flinch. He knew that these men would probably relieve the women of their wage packet as soon as they were home, perhaps by force, and be off to the pub to drink their fill, but there was little he could do about that. That particular problem needed to be addressed by educators, but he had made a start, and it gave him a clearer conscience.

Some of the younger women, those who were unmarried, would be strong enough to refuse their father or brother, or whichever male patriarch kept them in slavery, and would be able to have some sort of of choice over their own lives. He could only hope but in the meantime, he must continue to build on his plans.

As a mill owner, he was able to offer his workers education and used the local, newly built Co-op lecture rooms and library to hold lessons for the betterment of their minds and to tap into the creativity that was lying dormant beneath the surface. He was already well thought of by the working people of the town and now he was risking that reputation and gaining the enmity of the other mill owners and members of the establishment to nail his colours to the mast in this way.

This Thursday evening, he stands in contemplation, looking at the still workroom, watching the late-night cleaners sweeping the long-handled brushes under the Fustian benches to remove the lint in preparation for the next day's work. He noted the marks on the floor where women had walked back and forth the length of the long tables, cutting the silk. The floorboards were worn deep by the steady beat of their feet across the years. Fustian Cutters walked up to 25 miles a shift, up and down this floor and he would be hanged if he would give their wages to a man just because they were women. The enormity of the injustice was his driving force.

Women were equal to men and should be treated with the same dignity and respect. Women were held in this kind of enforced slavery by a system that made them chattels to their fathers who gave them away to their husbands like farm animals. To work and slave and produce at the will of men, he would not be a party to it or allow it to have any place in his life or in his mill.

I will do what I can to help them here and I will campaign and finance every effort to bring about female emancipation. This world will be a better place when women are afforded an equal place in society he thought as he turned and left the building.

Ben liked Congleton. Its population was small yet large enough for him to pick and choose his workers and he chose the smartest, most willing-to-learn women. He paid them decent wages and offered them the opportunity to advance themselves via education with his programme of lectures and lessons at the Co-op Hall.

"Education is the most important tool a women can have in order to break free of the tyranny of male oppression" in the words of his dear friend and ally Annie Besant.

****

The following day finds Ben standing in Priesty Fields, and his mind is a turmoil of emotion. He is looking across to Astbury Church and yet not really seeing the sight. That morning, he had received some devastating news at breakfast time, one of his workers, Grace Smallwood had died suddenly overnight.

At first, he thought that her husband, an abusive brute, had in one of his drunken rages, attacked her. She had often come into work bruised and he had asked his leading hand to keep a special eye on her, but no it wasn't that. The leading hand, whose trust he had gained and kept him appraised of the personal lives of the women, had told him that she had paid a local woman to terminate an unwanted pregnancy, and something had gone horribly wrong.

She had worked her last shift the day before; had probably been in horrible pain all the way through it. He imagined her walking back and forth cutting the silk and all the time walking against, what must have been excruciating agony. Back and forth, bleeding out her life's blood for twelve long hours and then apparently, going home to her husband and five children, cooking them a meal before going at last to bed, where she died in the early hours. Her drunken husband had slept through the whole thing, awakening to a blood-soaked bed and a dead wife.

This was the lot of working-class women. His eyes filled with tears, and he felt the burden of her death and the five children who had lost their mother and breadwinner.

"Oh, her useless husband! Men, men, men, why can't you see what's right under your noses? The love of a woman like Grace is a jewel beyond compare. She was so loyal; she knew that I knew she was being abused but would never say a bad word against the perpetrator. That monster abused her body and felt it was his right to use her in any way he wished. He worked her for his own shallow profit."

She knew that I knew she was being abused but would never say a bad word against the perpetrator. I must do some research, proper research, there has been some pioneering work in the field of family planning; Annie and Charles seem to know about such things, I will contact them and ask their help and advice.

Ben had no idea how it worked but he simply had to find out and include healthcare and family planning in his lectures at the Co-op Hall. He could not bear the idea of more of his workers ending up like poor Grace.

Ben

Why do people have to be so secretive about the reproductive system? It is utterly ridiculous. To be so frightened of mentioning menstruation and procreation keeps people in ignorance. Young girls taken by surprise by their own bodies are terrified by what is happening to them and have nowhere to turn to ask the many questions they need answering. And men, well where do I start with that situation?

I have been in correspondence with Annie and reading her many suggested books and papers, on the subject of the human reproductive system, so I hope I am becoming quite an expert on the topic. I must give some lectures; men need to know this as well as women; just as soon as I am absolutely sure of all the facts, I will write a scheme of work to teach the topic at the Coop Hall. If I can help women to be free of the tyranny of yearly maternity, I will be very pleased with my life.

I have also been studying my dogs and cats. Their menstrual patterns are exactly the same as humans, they bleed mate and get pregnant. Surely, it's simple, if a woman does not have congress when she is bleeding, she will not get pregnant, there must therefore be a "safe period" the middle days of the cycle where pregnancy is impossible. If ovulation occurs when the woman menstruates, as it does with dogs and cats, and cows and all other mammals, then that is the time to abstain from sexual congress. Just as we keep our dogs separate when they are in season and bleeding, the process must be identical in humans.

Surely, it's as basic as that. We just need to educate ourselves about that fact and practice abstinence when menstruating.

CHAPTER 13
Moody Hall 1867

After all the hard work and upheaval of the move, here she was, standing in the entrance hall of Moody Hall in Congleton. Everything unpacked, everything clean and tidy, staff arriving tomorrow and girls arriving on Monday.

She was so tired but there were still two hours before she could allow herself the luxury of sleep. Mary her stepmother was busy in the kitchen preparing them a late meal, so Elizabeth took the opportunity of taking a walk in the rear garden. The sky was paling into a turquoise, summer evening and the birds had taken to their roosts in preparation for the coming night, bats swooped in their energetic excitement; she could hear their chirps as they flew.

It was a small garden but had some large trees through which she wandered to the very edge where the Howty Brook ran merrily. As she watched the water flow, she soaked up the much-desired peace. She inhaled the evening air in great, refreshing gulps and stood in thought, contemplating the future, and wondering what Congleton had in store for her.

The golden light from the setting sun, cast a strange glow on the scene. It turned Elizabeth's figure to bronze and Mary Wolstenholme, catching sight of her through the kitchen window, stopped dead and stared. How strange Elizabeth looked; it felt to her like a portent of things to come, a time when Elizabeth would be so famous that she would be immortalised in bronze.

****

Congleton was a very different place to Roe Green, although, like Manchester, it was literally peppered with mills, these were small silk mills, not the huge cotton mills of her former Lancashire home.

She listed in her mind the things she had to do, her number one priority was getting the curriculum for the school up and running. She needed to identify people in the area who could aid her with that and the people who could also help with her wider, campaigns and projects.

She had already been advised to seek out Ben Elmy who was a former schoolmaster and an ardent feminist, who now owned three small mills here. She had been advised to meet him as he held similar views to herself and was working on an education programme for the workers in the town. Apparently, Mr Elmy pays his women their wages and refuses to hand it to any husband or father, he had made enemies of the other mill owners for this, she was reliably informed. This was the kind of thing she loved to hear; she would start her enquiries tomorrow.

However, she was overtaken by events when the following morning, immediately after breakfast, just as she was preparing to sit at her writing desk, the doorbell rang, and she heard her stepmother's footsteps echoing in the hallway as she hurried to answer it.

Expecting it to be the postman with the expected last-minute delivery of books and paper, she sat down to settle into her morning's work, leaving the delivery in Mary's capable hands. So, it surprised her greatly when Mary came into her study and said a gentleman named Mr Ben Elmy was in the drawing room and had called hoping to see her.

"Thank you, Mother, tell him I'll be there shortly."

She gave Mary a few minutes to complete the task then rose from her chair, pulled herself up to her full height of 4 ft 10 ins and walked slowly across the room. She opened the door to the drawing room and saw a dark figure standing in the shaft of sunlight which was streaming through the French window behind him.

"Miss Wolstenholme, what a pleasure to meet you. I have heard so much about your work. Please allow me to introduce myself, I am Ben Elmy, and I am interested in the education of women and girls, and I am thrilled you have moved your school here to Congleton. I am hoping we can work together for the betterment of women and humanity in general, but forgive me, I'm talking in a rush."

He extended his hand and walked towards her out of the blinding light, and she saw him properly for the first time. Smiling face; warm, earnest eyes, he looked to Elizabeth to be open and honest. Something about this man made her feel instantly relaxed and as she took his hand and smiled in return, her fate was sealed. Of course, she didn't know that then, but she warmed to him: at that moment, some deep, natural instinct recognised a kindred spirit.

"Can I suggest that we take a walk? It's a beautiful May morning and I want to hear everything about your work and aspirations, and I'd like to tell you about some of the things I've been doing for local women. Although I do know a lot about your work with Mrs Butler, William Stead and Annie Bessent on the Contagious Disease question, and I have read some of your pamphlets and writings on women's education and enfranchisement. Have you time to spare or shall I return at a later more convenient date?"

Elizabeth should have refused and asked him for a more formal meeting, but there was something about this man that intrigued her, and she wanted to hear what he had to say, so instead they set out on the first of many walks in the lush countryside surrounding their town.

The morning rushed towards the afternoon and still they walked. They talked of the vote, education, secularism; the list was endless and so far, there was nothing they disagreed on. Eventually, they had to return to Moody Hall as there was so much work to be done but they parted reluctantly with plans to meet again as soon as possible to discuss the possibility of Elizabeth teaching some lessons at the Coop Hall and Ben teaching likewise at Moody Hall.

****

A month later they are walking in the June sunlight along the banks of the River Dane. It is Sunday so the world is at prayer but not Ben and Elizabeth. They had quickly established that they were both Secularists and didn't believe in any personal God, so it was their day off.

Elizabeth had developed a deep respect for this man, he was a thinker and an ardent feminist but also a romantic poet and writer. She liked him very much but was finding their developing relationship challenging.

"So, you see Elizabeth, unless a woman has full control over her own bodily functions, she can never, ever be truly free. She will always be at the whim of her husband, and he will control every aspect of her life. If he is a good and loving man and treats her as an equal, then there is no great problem but if he treats her as his chattel and exercises complete control over her, he can force unwanted pregnancy after unwanted pregnancy and, under the law of the land as it now stands, she has no rights whatsoever, she is no better than a farm animal. Why she can even be raped and beaten and has nowhere to go as English Law affords a married woman no protection from such treatment."

She looked at his earnest face and remained silent. She agreed completely and had often voiced similar opinions, but this feeling from a man was a complete revelation to her. She was totally euphoric; Ben was speaking, and she was hanging on his every word. He listened to her and valued everything she said but no, no, no this was not going to happen to her, she could not allow it to happen to her!

What was this feeling? She had never felt anything like it before. It was the stuff of silly romantic novels. Young girls being tricked by men into thinking they were in love! Giving up their freedom to become the slaves of tyrant males; it was a very powerful feeling. If this was love, then she suddenly understood that it was all-consuming and rational thought could easily be abandoned. It was animalistic, basic and she could see how it could be used to control people if one person felt it and the other did not. Just tell tales of true love and happy-ever-after and a woman could easily be beguiled, convinced that this is where happiness and contentment lay. She must fight this at all costs, or she could find herself losing control and giving up everything she had ever fought for.

She closed her eyes and breathed in deeply and inwardly chanted her mantra, justice, justice, justice! Elizabeth Wolstenholme was having the biggest fight of her life thus far.

"Mr Elmy, Sir, I hear your reasoning and understand it fully, I agree in every detail, but I cannot spend any more time on this today. Let us return to Moody Hall where there are letters to write and classes to prepare."

Thus, she closed him down and was silent on their return journey. At Moody Hall she dismissed him rudely and did not invite him in for tea as had been their custom of late, leaving him to walk dejectedly away.

Mary stood and watched as Elizabeth entered alone, she had been used to serving them tea and cake. She watched open mouthed as Elizabeth removed her coat and climbed the stairs.

Elizabeth entered her room and stared at herself in the mirror. Her heart was in turmoil. Oh, poor Ben I have been so cruel, so rude, I hope he forgives me someday, but I simply cannot trust my feelings. I cannot allow myself to be put in this weak condition. Oh, my goodness, what is happening to me? Elizabeth, take care girl! This man is dangerous and could scupper your plans and take away your hard-won independence.

Be strong - justice, justice, justice.

Elizabeth

It had been my intention to cut him out of my life. Like the amputation of a diseased limb or organ, to take the scalpel and cut it, quickly and sharply; get it over and done with in one fell swoop: it isn't proving that easy.

What a strange feeling this is, I have loved people and animals all my life, I have truly known love, but this is all-consuming; on a totally different scale I cannot sleep without dreaming of him, when I try to write, he invades my thoughts. I find myself thinking, I wonder what Ben would say; it is utterly ridiculous.

I do hope this infatuation passes soon, for it is making me feel quite unwell, and yet there is a strange beauty in it.

Is this real "love"? I hardly dare think!

CHAPTER 14
The Courtship

Ben

I simply do not know what I did wrong, but it must have been something serious. I feel like such a fool! There she was the most interesting and beautiful woman I have ever met. She was in my grasp, and I lost her: it was almost mid-sentence! Oh, Elizabeth what did I do to offend you?

I will not give up, I will win her heart and together we can make a difference, but without her at my side I fear, I cannot possibly go on. I never realised how much I needed a soulmate before now, but I have very quickly established that I most certainly do and that my personal soulmate is Elizabeth Wolstenholme.

Oh, my love, do not forsake me, my heart aches for you. I am raked fore and aft!

For the next three weeks, Elizabeth attempted to rebuff Ben. He would call at Moody Hall but would not be allowed to see Elizabeth. He left calling cards and numerous invitations, but all were ignored. Eventually, Ben left an invitation she simply could not refuse. He invited her to dinner at his home with some distinguished guests.

She hadn't known that Ben was acquainted with Charles Bradlaugh and Annie Besant, so the invitation took her breath away. She had ducked back from the window when she saw his figure walking deliberately towards Moody Hall that morning. He had knocked and asked politely to see Elizabeth but Edith the maid, had followed her instructions and told him that Elizabeth was too busy to see visitors. So, he had left the invitation for her attention. From her vantage point, she had watched his dejected retreat. *Poor Ben, he must be so confused but he is very persistent; I cannot trust myself.*

Edith knocked and entered and handed her the invitation and upon reading it a flood of excitement caused her to draw in her breath. She raised her hand to her mouth as she gasped. Startled by the sound, Edith turned from the door and with eyes wide said, "Bad news Miss?"

"No, no, not at all; good news in fact, very good news." Edith's face relaxed and broke into a smile. "Tell cook I won't be at home for dinner on Friday."

This was the point where her defences began to crumble.

****

They were seated round the table at The Low, Ben's home. Four earnest people, deep in conversation, each listening intently as the others spoke. Elizabeth was charmed to find that Annie called Charles CB and Charles called Annie AB. They had a wonderful relationship, so relaxed, so equal and such fun.

They were busy discussing religion and how it was devised by men to control people. How intelligent people saw through it, but the uneducated masses believed it to be true and therefore policed each other to keep the masters, royalty and gentry in their elevated, 'God-given' positions.

"Once they have convinced the populace that they are in their position of grandeur and riches by the will of some imaginary deity, then they can keep their exalted positions and the people in their perceived places as their servants. They will even fight and kill each other to defend the hierarchy and so keep their masters lording it over them.

The fact that women are hardly named in the Bible and when they are they are the property of men, maintains the status quo. It is totally illogical, but people have been persuaded and even raised from birth to believe that the Bible is the word of God, so anything written there is sacrosanct.

Most people can't or won't read a Bible, so it is not checked or questioned at all. They simply accept the circular logic that is presented to them as fact from childhood onward.

God exists because the Bible says he does. But who wrote the Bible? God wrote the Bible. How do you know God wrote the Bible? The Bible says so." Charles guffawed with laughter and threw his head back; he was very entertaining.

He was a large man, some 6 foot 6 inches and a good 3 foot across the shoulders; physically quite imposing. Elizabeth couldn't imagine anyone standing in Charles Bradlaugh's way: she was hanging on his every word with awe.

Annie was very interested in Elizabeth's work, asked many knowledgeable questions about her curriculum, and nodded in agreement. They had corresponded already in their mutual work on the repeal of the Contagious Diseases Act campaign, and Elizabeth had of course heard both Annie and Charles speak at the Free Trade Hall, but this was their first proper, personal meeting.

Annie was particularly interested in Elizabeth's embryonic idea about teaching biology and including family planning as a necessity. It was one of Annie's chief interests and she was very knowledgeable on the subject feeling that it was a key element to female emancipation. By the end of the evening, Elizabeth felt that she had found two very good, like-minded friends and was even more enamoured of the Free Love movement through her observation of their relationship. This was the first time that she had realised that Ben was also a member, and she just couldn't help herself warming to him even more.

Elizabeth announced it was time for her to go and Ben rose to see her out, but she insisted that she was quite capable of finding her carriage herself and left him standing in the dining room with his guests. She collected her coat and left the house via the front door, but Annie left the dining room and joining her, walked with her to her carriage.

"Elizabeth, do you dislike Ben so much that you will not even allow him to say a formal goodnight to you?"

"It is not that Annie; I do not dislike him, quite the opposite. I am very fond of him, he is an admirable man, but I cannot allow myself to enter a relationship with a member of the opposite sex, it would distract me too much from my work and I have too much to lose. It would jeopardise my school as I would lose my reputation among other things; it's simply too big a step for me to take. I have no time for it and it's not fair of me to encourage something I could never give my whole self to. He is a lovely man and very erudite and knowledgeable, I very much want him as my friend and I'm happy to have him as a working colleague, but never as a lover."

She was staring deeply into Annie's eyes as she spoke, and Annie returned her stare. She held a thoughtful silence before answering softly. "What a dilemma you have Elizabeth for it is obvious that Ben Elmy is very enamoured of you." Then she lightened the moment by saying "all work and no play makes Liz a dull girl" and with that, she giggled and added, "I couldn't survive without my bedtime with CB" and she winked cheekily at Elizabeth.

Elizabeth drew in her breath sharply and her eyes widened in shock, then covering her mouth she started to giggle and then to fully laugh as she climbed into her carriage. Once seated she leaned her head through the open window to say a final farewell, but Annie reached out her hand and grasped Elizabeth's.

"Be advised by me Elizabeth, some things happen only once in a lifetime and are more precious than gold. Be careful lest you miss an amazing opportunity by trying to hold onto respectability and social standing. Men like Ben Elmy are few and far between."

"Mrs Besant, may I remind you of our difference in age? I think I have been on this planet a few years longer than you and should not need to take worldly advice on such subjects."

"You may be older than me Elizabeth, but you have not had the experience of men and the world of men that I have had in my few short years; but come let us part friends."

With that Annie smiled again and Elizabeth relaxed, realising that she had flown off the handle again; she fully recognised that this was an imperfection that had caused her a lot of trouble. "Yes, yes of course, forgive me I'm turning into a grumpy old woman and I'm not yet 40! Forgive me Annie dear I am on the horns of a dilemma, as you have perceived."

They both laughed and relaxed, neither wanted to lose their friendship because of a passing conversation at the end of a most wonderful evening.

Elizabeth drew back into her carriage and the driver moved off. Waving through the window she began the short journey back to Moody Hall. She had much to think about and dissect and her head was in turmoil.

Elizabeth

What a glorious evening, what brilliant people, I could have stayed and chatted all night. Annie and Charles seem to have a really wonderful relationship and they obviously love each other so very much. They are so free, so self-assured, so well-grounded in their beliefs.

Ben was his usual delightful self also: I am undone, for I would dearly love to have such a relationship with Mr Elmy but I cannot, I have too much to lose. Annie's parting remark though; what am I to make of that? She is a very perceptive young woman.

****

As the weeks and months progressed Ben slowly, slowly worked on Elizabeth. Making himself a key confidante and counsellor in her life. He was never long away from Moody Hall and Elizabeth's presence. They worked together on her many campaigns and Ben wrote letters, petitions, pamphlets, and a multitude of poems that delighted her. It was his one aim in life to win her over and form a team that could change the world for women and girls. He was as driven as she was, and he was a rare thing; her intellectual equal.

Ben entered the room, he had come to discuss her upcoming lecture on Lord Tennyson, it was scheduled for later that week. The posters were up, and the excitement was growing among the mill workers.

"Good morning, Elizabeth, why the sad face?"

Elizabeth forced a smile. "Oh, nothing Ben, I'm just struggling with winning my new intake of girls. It's not that they are badly behaved or disrespectful, far from it they are the epitome of good behaviour and good manners, no I am struggling to break through the barrier of apathy which consumes them. They are a particularly difficult group, like a brick wall, each one off in her own personal world, a world where I am failing to be admitted."

She sighed and looked down at a piece of written work on her desk. "Take this for instance" she flicked the page on her desk, "Sarah Boardman, an intelligent young woman who should be devouring books and knowledge but who has been stuck into the mould of "agreeable, obedient daughter" and seems to have no desire to break free, indeed, cannot even see that she needs to break free or even where that freedom lies. All she is interested in is fashion and hairstyles; it is all so very discouraging."

Ben walked towards her placing his hat and walking cane on the settle as he passed. "This doesn't sound like you Elizabeth. Are you saying you are having difficulty inspiring these girls? If so, I find that difficult to understand as you are truly inspirational; a role model par excellence."

"That's exactly what I am saying Ben; have you any ideas?"

A serious look crossed his face as he drew a deep breath and began to speak "Elizabeth, you know how we have spoken about how one of the main needs for girls' is sex education; how girls need to know all about sexual congress and its consequences? Well, I've been working on a booklet that I think could be used as a teaching scheme for your girls. I've been giving it a great deal of thought and I think we could start with asking one of the young mothers at the mill to come into the school and bring her baby. If we find the right willing girl to come in and be open and honest, she could tell your young ladies what childbirth is like. Perhaps one of the women from your women's group? You know them well you could choose just the right one. You could then use your nature rambles to point out the things in nature that I have used as illustrations in the booklet."

"That would wake them up Ben, that would shock them out of their reverie, make them think about what their future lives are going to entail. I think you have something; the girls would never go back and tell their parents about such lessons. I declare it also solves another worry I have; my younger girls know nothing about menstruation, nothing at all. I have in just the last month alone, had no less than 3 hysterical, terrified young girls thinking that they are dying because of their first issue of blood. We could devise a comprehensive scheme of work to solve this problem for the girls. It would help to shock them out of their catatonia and make them think about what they really want to do with their lives."

Ben was enthused "I will send my carriage back to The Low and ask my servant to bring my documentation. I will run you through it and we can perfect it together."

He left the room to ask Joseph to take his carriage back to The Low and ask his housekeeper to retrieve the large brown folder from his desk. The one marked "The Human Flower" and then returned to Elizabeth's study.

Elizabeth's demeanour had changed completely. "Thank you, dearest Ben, that's just what I needed, someone to see through the fog and point me in the right direction. You are truly my right-hand man."

Ben laughed but was secretly very pleased that he had received the desired outcome. His plan to make himself indispensable to this amazing little woman was coming along apace. He was determined to win her over, heart and mind.

The following weeks and months were difficult for Elizabeth, holding Ben off was getting more and more problematic. Her cast-iron resolve was weakening by the hour and only sheer bloody-mindedness was keeping her from opening her heart completely to Ben.

In the end, on one cold, crisp morning shortly before Christmas, Ben brought up the subject.

"Let me be honest with you Elizabeth, I have never met a woman like you. I have never had a meeting of minds that is so complete and conclusive. I believe with all my heart that you are my soulmate, and that the Universe intends that we should spend the rest of our lives together."

They were in the parlour at The Low, Ben's home. Elizabeth had been across for tea and a discussion about the lecture she was to give at the Co-op Hall. Ben had used the occasion to broach the topic she had been avoiding.

She sat looking at him in silence; every one of her nerves was stretched to breaking point. She was both horrified and yet mesmerised. She had known in her heart that this moment was going to arrive but now here it was, and she didn't know how to respond.

Ben came and knelt at her feet and lifting her hand to his lips he said.

"Elizabeth you are my world, my absolute reason to be alive. Darling, I would do anything for you, reach up into the sky and pull down the moon and the stars if that's what you require of me. I truly believe that together you and I can change the world for women everywhere. I ask you Elizabeth to enter a Free Union with me, and I promise that I will respect and love you till my dying breath. Just think together we will become Wolstenholme and Elmy the most formidable fighting force in the Universe."

Elizabeth was frozen to the spot. What was she supposed to do now? She drew in her breath and pulled her eyes away from Ben, but not for long, returning them to his she replied. "Oh, Ben! What can I say, do you know what this will mean for us, for me in particular? We will be shunned even more than we are now as Secularists and Socialists! I will be a fallen woman. You will probably be just fine, there are different rules for men, but I will lose my school; parents will not want their daughters in the hands of someone they perceive to be living in sin."

"Elizabeth why should nonsense like that bother us? They are chattering about us already! We can stand on our convictions and stare down the establishment, we have nothing to fear, and we will be an example and a strength to women everywhere. It is swings and roundabouts what you lose one way you gain another. The bottom line is, are you up to the challenge? Will you pick up the gauntlet? Will you fight for justice for women with me and will you be my equal partner in a Free Union?"

She stared into his earnest eyes and thought briefly before her eyes closed and her face relaxed. "Yes! Yes of course, there is no other path I can take for I love you Ben, completely and utterly. I have tried to fight it, but I am hopeless before the onslaught of my own feelings and desires; I am powerless before them. I too feel that the Universe has decreed that we do a brave and wonderful thing."

Ben beamed and taking her into his arms, kissed her deeply before saying, "Then let us plan our Wedding Day. We will say our own vows and make our own promises in true Wolstenholme and Elmy style. We'll set a date, we'll have flowers and good friends in attendance."

Elizabeth's heart was filled with happiness as she thought for a moment and then replied, "let's do it on the banks of the Dane, before men and all nature, in the sunshine, in our own special way, in our own special place?"

Ben threw back his head and laughed "Oh yes, my darling, that's perfect, absolutely perfect, let's do it and do it soon."

So it came to pass that on a bright April morning when the birds were building their nests and displaying their finery to attract a mate; in the golden morning air Elizabeth, wearing a new summer dress and carrying a bunch of spring flowers walked with Ben to the banks of the Dane. They were accompanied by a small group of true friends but no priest, vicar or minister of any sort; they were doing it just the way they planned.

Ben went first:

"Elizabeth, you are my soulmate and best friend. You have taken my heart, my soul and my mind. Everything I am is yours, everything I own is yours, you are the very air I breathe, without you I am nothing. We are a true meeting of minds, equal in all things. From this day on you are my one and only; we will stick like glue, and I will love you till I die."

Elizabeth responded:

"Ben my dearest, do not talk of glue, for glue is such an ugly substance. Glue is sticky, dirty stuff and speaks of broken things: shattered shards of once perfect pottery or papers torn apart. No, my darling, we have no need of glue for we fit perfectly together like jigsaw pieces and yet stronger even than that; like a craftsman's perfectly made dove-tail joint. We were made for each other and once placed together we will never come apart, no matter what pressure is applied. We are perfect for the task in hand, together we will bring hope, truth and justice."

So that was the day that Elizabeth Wolstenholme and Benjamin John Elmy became one before all nature and the Universe and a few close friends. Their vows were heartfelt and true, and they needed no piece of official paper to attest to the fact.

CHAPTER 15
Christmas at Moody Hall 1868

Elizabeth

A group of girls given into my care and I know what I want to teach them, but I also know they have parents who want them taught a certain way. They are liberal enough to allow a few new ideas, but they are not liberal enough to allow their daughters to be taught anything that is not based on Christian principles and certainly will not be happy if I get them to think outside the box on the subject of God and Creation.

From the group of pupils I have, it looks to me as though the parents have identified that the girls are intelligent and need more than a governess can provide, but anything progressive enough to look and sound radical would be frowned upon. I have a dilemma it seems.

I have to go slowly; feel my way gently and carefully introduce new subjects into their thought processes. The problem is these middle-class girls are trained to sit around and sew and embroider to the point where they now have no interest in anything at all. Their every conversation is dresses and ribbons or some such trivia.

They have the basics of reading and writing but have no interest in any book other than the Bible, which has been forced upon them and which they read as though it is the truth without absorbing what it is actually saying or questioning its contents. They do of course devour the shallow women's journals that their mothers send from time to time; great prizes they pass around excitedly. I am struggling to see how I can lift them from this shallow state; turn them aside from the path they are on and break this cycle of waste.

Today Victoria Montague asked me why they had to go on the nature ramble when it was raining; apparently, they had seen plenty of trees before. Dear girl, she appears lazy intellectually but really, the truth is she has been beaten down by the societal training she has received from birth and the subliminal message she has taken on that life for a girl is a tedious thing and marriage and children her only option.

In my school girls are allowed to run about and get dirty, encouraged to be inquisitive and ask questions. Just like boys, they are allowed the *intellectual freedom to be curious, to question and to sample everything life throws their way. My girls are not trained to sit quietly and sew a fine seam. It is my job to draw them out and remove twelve years of bad influence?*

****

The girls were excited and getting ready for Christmas most were going home but some, whose parents were abroad, were spending the festive season at school in Congleton. Harriet had also come to stay, so it was a happy bunch of females who were preparing for a Christmas holiday like no other.

December weather in Congleton that year was strangely warm, Elizabeth couldn't remember a December like it, warm but very windy and it rained and rained and rained. The girls were disappointed as they longed for snow so they could take to the meadows and build snowmen and slide on the frozen Macclesfield Canal, but it wasn't to be. Instead, they were confined indoors but Elizabeth kept them entertained with her storytelling.

One evening early in December, Sarah Boardman said that they should turn one of Elizabeth's stories into a play and perform it on New Year's Eve and all present thought it a superb idea.

Much discussion took place as to which of Elizabeth's stories should be used and they couldn't decide. Finally, Elizabeth said "Why don't we do a traditional story?"

"Good idea, but which shall we use. Maybe Mother Goose or Cinderella?" suggested Sarah.

"Why not Punch and Judy? We haven't a huge number of players, and we do have my little dog, Sammy; surely, he can play Toby?"

"Oh, but Elizabeth! Punch and Judy is a horrible story about a man who ill-treats his poor wife and children. That's not a suitable story at all" cut in Harriet in alarm.

"Think about it. We can re-write the story to depict Judy as getting the better of Punch and Punch being repentant. Use your imagination girls, could that policeman not arrest horrible old Punchinello and help poor Judy to escape his clutches? When that feckless Punch sees that he no longer has control, he will hardly know what to do. Come, get your heads working let's write the play."

So, the playwriting and the making of the props and costumes kept the girls busy over the next few rainy days whilst Elizabeth, Harriet and Mary planned the food and festivities.

****

Christmas Eve dawned just as wet and windy as the previous days and would have been extremely miserable for the girls, except they hardly noticed as they concentrated all their energies on their play.

Elizabeth pulled them away from their theatricals in the mid-afternoon to decorate the hall and dining room and their excitement grew as a very wet Ben arrived with a new innovation, a huge Fir Tree which he placed in a tub in the hall. The girls spent the rest of the day decorating it with the white paper angels and colourful paper chains they made.

After the evening meal, they all sat around the tree in the hall whilst Ben carefully lit the candles. Then they sang carols, drank fruit cup and ate mince pies. Each girl had a stocking to hang by the Christmas Tree and there was much giggling that night as they settled down excitedly to try and sleep.

It was warm and cosy in Moody Hall that night, though the wind and the driving rain made it far from a silent night. Elizabeth, Ben, Mary and Harriet sat around the roaring fire in the drawing room.

"What a great success your tree is Ben." said Mary.

"They are quite the thing now Mrs Wolstenholme, most houses have one these days, I'm surprised the fashion has escaped you for so long!"

"At my dizzy age, I am hardly the person to ask on matters of fashion Mr Elmy" she said with a laugh.

"I am so impressed with the script the girls have written Elizabeth, that really was an inspirational idea of yours. It's got the girls thinking about the Punch and Judy story and the way they have thought and talked about the issues it throws up has shown that you have managed to get through to these young women. Well done, Elizabeth," said Harriet.

"It's good then is it, Harriet?" asked Ben.

"It's more than good Ben, it's wonderful and makes me cry, which takes a lot."

"Why not open it to the public?" He looked at the women quizzically.

"I hadn't thought of that" Elizabeth answered but looked thoughtful as she considered it. "Do you think that people will be interested in a performance on New Year's Eve?"

"I do indeed, why don't we open the Co-op Hall? We can start advertising on Boxing Day. I'm sure lots of families would come along for an afternoon matinee."

Elizabeth and Harriet looked at each other and their excitement grew. "It would be a lovely surprise for the girls. I'm sure they would love to perform it to a live audience" smiled Elizabeth and Harriet and Mary nodded in agreement.

"We will announce it to them at Christmas Dinner, an extra little Christmas Present" said Elizabeth solemnly "Can I leave the arrangements regarding the Co-op Hall to you Ben?"

"Of course my dear, I live to serve."

The women laughed their appreciation.

Christmas Day 1868 was just like Christmas Eve, wet, windy and unseasonably warm. The girls were whispering and giggling from early morning as they waited in the dark to be allowed to get up and dressed to go downstairs to their stockings.

Elizabeth stood in the cool hall and listened to the wind blowing noisily around the chimney pots. She could smell the wonderful aroma of the pine tree mixed with the pomanders that the girls had made by pushing cloves into oranges and hanging the fruit from the tree among the white paper angels and multi-coloured paper chains. They had worked long throughout the week preparing them to deck the hall and dining room, so their perfume had permeated the whole of the ground floor. They looked and smelled so wonderful and also on the morning air, was the smell of bacon cooking in Mary's kitchen.

How lucky I am she thought as she surveyed her home, how happy I am here in my precious school. What more could I possibly want than I have right now at this moment?

Deep in her heart Elizabeth knew that the tenure of her school was ending. Parents would not like her relationship with Ben, she predicted that this was probably her last Christmas as a schoolteacher, but Ben, and their relationship was precious to her and if she couldn't have both him and her school then she would choose Ben.

She stood for a few minutes listening to the sounds of food preparation and girls chatting and giggling. She longed to stop time and remain here in this moment for the rest of her life. But then she suddenly thought, how selfish I am, there are women and girls living under the tyranny of male oppression, I must continue the fight for justice. So, shaking her head she struck the gong in the hall which signalled to the girls that they could begin their morning rituals and come down to breakfast and Christmas Stockings.

Her thoughts were suddenly disturbed by Mary entering from the kitchen door. "This weather is so unseasonable; it doesn't feel at all like Christmas, more like Mad March" she exclaimed.

The girls hardly noticed; they were too busy looking in their stockings. Each girl had soap, a hair slide, a small box of chocolates and an orange; they were well pleased.

They giggled through breakfast, then worked on their play whilst Mary, Harriet and Elizabeth worked on the Christmas Feast. A large turkey had been delivered early that morning and there was much work to be done getting it in the oven. The trimmings were many and time-consuming. Mary had prepared the pudding and the Christmas Cake many weeks before in October but there was a dinner that could not be cooked earlier. Hams and pies were baked ahead of time, but the vegetables had to be prepared and the turkey roasted.

Harriet took the girls to St Peter's Church for the Christmas Morning Carol Service, but Elizabeth and Mary remained behind, working hard in the kitchen.

By mid-afternoon, the girls were painting scenery and props and putting the finishing touches to some of the costumes. Practising their lines as they worked. The Punch and Judy had really captured their imaginations.

When Ben arrived at 6 pm the girls were all washed and smartly dressed and sitting in the dining room ready for the Christmas feast. He had brought each girl a fancy hairbrush, Harriet and Mary received some fine soaps and for Elizabeth a beautiful cameo brooch. It took Elizabeth's breath away and she immediately pinned it in the centre of her bodice at the collar. She declared it the finest thing she had ever seen or owned. She was rarely seen without it from that day on.

The elaborate meal was enjoyed by all and when it was over Ben questioned the girls about their play. They excitedly went into great detail and Sarah rushed away to bring one of the elaborate costumes she was so proud of sewing.

Ben listened intently and when their enthusiastic chatter waned slightly, he said "Ladies this all sounds so very fine. Surely such a production is far too grand to be played before such a small audience. Let me see, there will only be me, hopefully, and Mrs Wolstenholme and Miss Wolstenholme and Miss Arnold, such a pity." He shook his head and then, with a theatrical look of inspiration he looked at them excitedly. "I have an idea! How would you fine young ladies like to perform your play before the good people of Congleton, in the Co-op Hall no less?"

There was a silence and some strange looks and then, as they fully understood what he was saying, a squeal of delight went up. "Oh! Mr Elmy! Is that possible? Could we really?"

"Yes, it is possible for I, Benjamin John Elmy will make it possible. You had better get rehearsing, sewing, and painting, for you are going to star in the finest production that ever hit the fair town of Congleton."

The girls were beside themselves and their excitement grew and grew as the week between Christmas and New Year passed. Posters went up quickly on Boxing Day on every noticeboard in town and the shop windows and pubs. Tickets were bagged eagerly as the word spread of a surprise Christmas production.

The New Year's Eve production was a huge success. The good people of Congleton saw for the first time, the 'True Story of Punch and Judy' and applauded long and loud when Punch got his comeuppance and repented, promising to love and protect Judy if she would only forgive him and take him back.

This "True Story of Punch and Judy" became a regular feature in Congleton and is repeated at Town Fairs and events to this very day.

CHAPTER 16
Life in the Fast Lane

Ben was pontificating:

"Menstruation is a blight on the lives of women. I firmly believe that women's bodies will soon evolve to a better place where it does not exist. Men must be educated to understand that sexual intercourse should be avoided during the time of menstruation as this is the time when a woman's body is prepared to become pregnant. If a woman does not want maternity and motherhood, then a man should restrain himself at that time and sexual congress should only be practiced in the middle days of her cycle. It is the same in all mammals, dogs, cats, sheep, goats, and cows all are the same. Anyway, there is a much better way to make love, a psychic congress, where a true meeting of minds occurs, psychic love is far superior to physical love."

Elizabeth was trying to understand what exactly Ben was saying. She had long since bowed to his greater knowledge of sexual matters. He was a considerate and gentle lover, and she trusted him completely so left that side of things to him. She was not exactly ignorant of such things; hadn't she worked with prostitutes and mill women in her capacity as teacher and campaigner? It was the logistics of the thing, the anatomical details; Ben seemed to know what he was talking about, and Annie Bessent agreed so best leave it to him. She changed the subject. "Harriet is to be married."

"Ah it is as you suspected, her handsome farmer has finally thrown his hat into the ring." He smiled broadly.

"Yes, she is to be Harriet McIlquham, quite a tongue-twister. I shall have to practice the pronunciation; it would be a very bad show to mispronounce it when we next meet. I am very pleased for her Ben; although I know she has struggled with her conscience; she had sworn never to marry. I told her I would not hold it against her, and I am sure the Universe will not either."

"If it's what she truly wants then she should not rent her clothes and wear a hair shirt; it is surely more about what they decide as a couple. Mr McIlquham may feel that a marriage licence is important. If she is to swear to obey him, she had better start now." Ben laughed but Elizabeth shook her head and wagged her finger.

Elizabeth now spent most of her time teaching in the school and working on her campaigns but most of her nights she spent with Ben at The Low. They did not attempt to hide the situation and it very soon became common knowledge that they were living together in a Free Union. Of course, as Ben was a respected Mill Owner and a man, he was hardly if at all, affected by the situation, but Elizabeth was treated to the usual disrespect afforded to women who stepped outside the narrow confines of staid Victorian, Christian morality.

Over the last few weeks, Elizabeth had been approached by Millicent Fawcett, to become the first paid employee of the women's movement. She had worked with Millicent on several campaigns and Millicent was looking for a dedicated, hard-working woman to take the helm for lobbying Parliament.

Millicent was not pleased that Elizabeth was living openly with Ben, she was a committed Christian and considered Elizabeth to be "living in sin" but as Elizabeth was not the only member of the Free Love Movement and her work and intellect very much in demand, she was willing to turn a blind eye.

Elizabeth was torn. She discussed it at length with Ben. She was finding it harder and harder to teach her girls a curriculum that had Christianity as its basis, but the girls' parents expected it and when the news spread that she was living with Ben, she was probably going to lose her pupils anyway.

"You must accept the post Elizabeth, it's an open door to the heart of Westminster; just think what you can achieve?"

"But Ben you do realise that the post will require me to live the vast majority of my time in the capital?"

"There are trains, there are weekends, our love can survive the distance. Isn't the cause bigger than you and I?"

"I am very pleased with the movement I have created it goes from strength to strength, but I am very wary of accepting this offer of paid employment. Whereas all the women involved are united in the desire for equality for women, they are not united on several other important issues; Couverture for instance: some of the Christian, God-fearing members do not see the importance of women's property rights and rights over their own bodies. If I am a paid employee, then my voice on these matters may be curtailed. Millicent Fawcett as you know is deeply religious; I cannot have my thoughts and views censored in any way."

"I fully understand your reticence, but we have discussed this at length time and time again. You cannot keep the school going and spend half your time in London with your Kensington colleagues. The school is being criticised by parents because you quite rightly, refuse to teach Creation and Christianity as fact! Parents will start to withdraw their girls very soon, so Moody Hall's days are numbered anyway; it feels like a natural progression to me Elizabeth."

****

Ben is looking at her across the desk at Buxton House their newly acquired home in Buglawton. She is holding a letter from Millicent Fawcett setting out the terms and conditions of a job offer that on paper, is an absolute dream.

She read it again and then looked at Ben.

"I want to take this so much; however, I fear the influence of these women. They are alien to our ways and see the Free Love Movement as immoral. They will treat me as some sort of fallen woman. Everything in me cries out BEWARE: and yet I cannot refuse for it is such an important role and an obvious way of advancing the cause and achieving justice."

She pondered for a few moments longer and then drew in her breath, set her face like flint and went on determinedly. "I will write by return, accept the job, and then start planning to close Moody Hall at the end of the Summer Term. It will be with a very sad heart that I close my school, but needs must, and it has served me well both here and at Boothstown."

"A good decision dearest, a good decision and one I feel you will not regret. After all, you have already had several letters from parents enquiring if the rumours are true; it is only a matter of time before girls are withdrawn from Moody Hall. Better to go out on a high note rather than be driven out. I fully appreciate the post will mean less time here in Congleton with me, but the cause for equality is paramount. Absence makes the heart grow fonder my love, and I fully intend to make sure that it does in our case."

Elizabeth smiled in response but deep inside she had trepidation and a feeling of foreboding. She turned back to her work.

So it was that in 1873, Elizabeth Wolstenholme became *Scrutinizer of Parliamentary Practice for the Vigilance Association for the Defence of Personal Rights* and closed Moody Hall for good.

By the end of 1873 Elizabeth was working hard and had gained a high profile among the MPs in Westminster. She was studying constantly and had a vast knowledge of English Law and how it affected women. She was writing hundreds of letters a week and there wasn't a sitting MP that hadn't received correspondence from her. The MPs feared her because she was unrelenting and used her amazing knowledge of the law to the full. Her ability to articulate her points orally and in writing made her a formidable opponent; so afraid were they of a confrontation with Elizabeth Wolstenholme that they nick-named her, the Parliamentary Watchdog, and called her the Scourge of the Commons.

She was difficult to avoid and was often seen walking the corridors of the Palace of Westminster late into the night when important debates and votes were taking place; she was relentless and driven. This tiny powerhouse of a woman could not be turned away from her cause and her mantra, justice, justice, justice.

However, a whirlwind was on the horizon, something was about to strike Elizabeth, strike her hard and change her world.

CHAPTER 17
Battles and Disappointments

Elizabeth was on the train returning to Congleton, the first time she had been home for over a fortnight. She was very tired and longing to see Ben. She felt ill and had done so for the last few weeks and she knew exactly what the problem was.

As her train pulled into Congleton's immaculate station, she opened the door and peered out looking for Ben's figure; she was dismayed to find he wasn't there. Instead, Joseph, a young man from Eaton Mill who worked alongside Ben rushed towards her and took her bags with a huge smile on his face. "Just down here miss." He led the way to where the pony and trap were waiting. She was so disappointed it wasn't Ben.

"Where's Mr Elmy?"

"An extraordinary meeting of the Town Council or some such, over shortly Mr Elmy said."

She nodded and fighting back tears she allowed Joseph to help her into the trap.

On reaching Buxton House, Elizabeth's bags were taken in, and Joseph took the pony round to the stables at the rear of the house. Elizabeth went upstairs and removed her outside coat and shoes and lay on the bed to wait for Ben. She awoke to find the sky dark, and the hall and stairs lights on. She had been asleep for 3 hours!

"You're awake darling?" Ben's face came into view in the half-light of the bedroom and Elizabeth quickly sat up feeling guilty.

"Sorry yes, I fell asleep" and at this point, for some reason she didn't understand, she burst into tears.

Ben looked horrified "Elizabeth, dearest what on earth is the matter."

"Oh, Ben such a disaster, you are wrong, so very, very wrong."

"About what?"

"About the family planning, your "safe time" isn't safe at all. I fear that I am with child, and it's the last thing on earth I need or want at this time."

Ben's eyes grew huge; he stared speechless. He had no words to convey how absolutely dreadful he was feeling. How could he have been so stupid as to let this happen to her, how could he be so selfish? He felt like an animal, nothing better than the half-human, thoughtless, uneducated brutes that worked in his mills and subjected the women in their lives to this sort of brutality on a yearly basis.

He wanted to flee the house, he wanted to run through the front door, down Buxton Road and keep on running and running, but he recognised that this woman, his soulmate, the love of his life, needed him now. She was frightened, vulnerable and very weak and she needed his strength and protection. This was his time to step up to the mark, to prove himself to be the reliable, loving partner he had always strove to be.

"Elizabeth, dear heart, I am so sorry" and with that, he took her in his arms and held her close. "Do not fear, I am here, we will get through this. I know that parenthood was not something we ever planned or wanted but it is what it is. We will get through this, trust me darling we will, our love will get us through."

"I trusted you before and look at the mess I'm in!" She wailed out her misery and fear. "I am over 42 years old! I am far too old for this; childbirth killed my mother it will surely do for me now." She wept inconsolably.

Ben held his own misery in check, he knew that Elizabeth was very probably right. This was not his greatest day, not his finest hour and he felt the weight of it.

****

Elizabeth

What is wrong with me, shivering and shaking like I'm some young girl before the magistrates? How dare Millicent call me into her presence like a naughty schoolgirl before the head? Of course, I know what she wants, and I could well do without it at the moment. I am feeling so ill, so weak, this pregnancy business is no stroll in the park. I have vomited every morning and I feel bilious most of the day.

Rather than gaining weight and swelling up, I have lost weight and I'm shrinking. Ben is so worried about me, and I have to keep reminding myself and him that this is normal. He cannot believe how ill it is making me; neither can I to be honest. Now here I am for this further indignity; I really have not the patience.

I am well aware that Millicent and her cohorts have been chatting about me. Praying to their God for guidance I have no doubt. I wonder what their tiny minds have come up with.

Millicent Garrett Fawcett was a formidable woman, she disapproved of Elizabeth Wolstenholme's lifestyle, but she needed her brain power and endless, unrelenting energy. However, at this moment in time, she was disgusted with her.

"Elizabeth please come in. Take a seat dear you look like you need it. How are you keeping?" Millicent looked at Elizabeth with staged concern.

"I cannot lie Millicent; I have felt better but I'm sure you haven't called me to your office to discuss my health. Can we get down to whatever it is you want to discuss; I have very little time available, and I need to be back to my work as I'm hoping to travel home to Congleton this evening."

She was asserting herself and was well-practised at the art; she was older and wiser than Millicent and not willing to take any nonsense.

"Yes well, it's rather delicate I'm afraid. It has now become obvious to everyone that you are with child, and the fact that you are unmarried and with child is causing something of a scandal." She stared at Elizabeth unblinkingly.

"And what business is it of yours Millicent?" Elizabeth was rewarded when Millicent broke her gaze and looked down at her desk.

"The Committee met yesterday and has asked me to put it to you that you are bringing the women's movement and the cause into disrepute. You are a major figure in the public eye, and you are obviously very pregnant and very unmarried. You are being talked about in the press Elizabeth."

"Again, I ask, what business is it of yours or the committee's how I choose to live my life?"

Millicent pushed out her more than ample bosom, tilted her head back and looked down her nose at Elizabeth. "Oh, come on Elizabeth, you are a high-profile representative of the women's movement, a woman of advancing years and you move in high places; your condition is a scandal! How can you ask what business it is of ours?"

Elizabeth had no response, she realised that as difficult as this was, Millicent had a point and was not going to change her staunch Christian beliefs to accommodate Elizabeth and Ben's belief in Free Love.

"So, what are you proposing? What do you suggest I do? Things are what they are, you need me and I'm having a child; can we not find a way forward to our mutual benefit? At this moment in time, things have been reversed: I need your support and not the other way round."

Millicent let all the stiffness leave her body and relaxed. "There may be a possible course of action. After a long discussion, it was decided that if you were to marry Mr Elmy there may well be a way forward, a saving of face as it were; a way by which the women of the movement may regain some of the respect, they once had for you."

There was a long silence as the two women stared at each other across the desk. Elizabeth broke it. "Let me get this clear, you were happy enough for me to work tirelessly for the cause whilst I was openly living with Ben in a Free Union, but as soon as that Union bears fruit, I am beyond acceptance and my life has somehow become disgusting to you. You are now trying to force me to toe the line of your beliefs so that I can keep my job and remain in "polite society?" She paused for a second and drew a deep breath. "I'll have you know Millicent that Ben and I have never been, nor ever will be in "polite society" and I suggest you have sold me a dog."

"Be reasonable Elizabeth: think of the women!"

"Think of the women? Think of the women? Millicent, I never think of anything but the women. Every waking hour, I think of the women! I'm appalled that you have turned on me this way."

"No one has turned on you Elizabeth, you have brought it all upon your own head by your flagrant disobedience to God. Your life with Ben Elmy is a disgrace and you walked openly into it."

Elizabeth rose to her feet, lifted her chin, and pulled back her shoulders. "I will pretend I did not hear that. However, I note that you have shown your true mind. I would like you to consider this Mrs Fawcett. You seem to think that because you have an imaginary friend you can demand respect from others and that people should give way to your strong beliefs, well I too expect respect for the things that I think and believe. Your God is of no more importance to me than the Islamic God or the half a million Hindu Gods that plague this earth. I know that you will agree with me about the latter two being imaginary, but I have simply gone one God further, I don't believe in your God either and I believe that he is as imaginary as all the rest. You get no respect from me for your beliefs Millicent, as you show me none for mine. I will now return to Congleton and my home with Ben and upon my return to London we will meet again to discuss the future."

Millicent, red in the face, rose and opened her mouth to speak but Elizabeth was halfway through the door and response seemed pretty useless at this time. She was forced to watch as the door closed softly. She noted that Elizabeth, even in anger, never slammed a door or even shut it noisily. She felt bad but also self-righteous; she was doing God's work and sometimes one had to be ruthless; her reward was in heaven. She sat back down, stone-faced but unrepentant in the face of Elizabeth's perceived blasphemy.

Elizabeth felt faint and needed to find a public bench to sit on to recover her senses. She was angry beyond words, how dare they, how dare they, she railed in her head. She must get back to Ben, he would know what to do.

****

It was with a heavy heart that Elizabeth returned to Congleton that afternoon and it was well past sunset when she arrived after the eight-hour train ride. It was unplanned so there was no pony and trap to meet her, and she had to walk from the station to Buxton House.

She rang the doorbell and Sally opened it and gasped in surprise.

"Madam, we weren't expecting you till tomorrow night. Give me that bag, you look tired out."

She took Elizabeth's bag and her outdoor coat in the hall, noted the black rings beneath her eyes and watched as Elizabeth almost staggered into the drawing room.

"Where's Mr Elmy?"

"Not back from the mill yet. I'm expecting him shortly. You're just in time for the evening meal."

"Thank you I'll go freshen up."

When Ben arrived home half an hour later, she had recovered enough to be sitting in the drawing room with a cup of tea. Over their evening meal, she regaled Ben with the happenings of the morning and the ultimatum given to her by the women, her so-called, sisters.

Ben just stared at her as she spoke. He couldn't believe what he was hearing. "How dare they, what right or authority do they have to do this to us?"

"God's apparently" she retorted.

Ben rolled his eyes and they fell silent over their meal after which they retired to the drawing room, all this time, deep in thought.

"There is no obvious way out of this Elizabeth, the only possibility of you continuing in your role is to capitulate and marry. I can see no other way, for they will surely dismiss you if you remain unmarried and pregnant."

"But Ben it is against everything we have ever stood for; it should not be something we are forced to do!"

"I know, I know, but perhaps if we see it as yet another sacrifice for the cause, perhaps we can just do the distasteful thing and get it over with?"

She stared at him and then looked down at her cup. "Ben, I do not want to do this, I really, really don't, and in all honesty, I don't think it will be good enough for these sanctimonious, Christian women. I think I may well end up unemployed anyway."

"I fear you may well be right dearest. I must be honest with you though if there is a small chance does it really make that much difference to us?"

"Of course not, but that's hardly the point is it?"

After a short silence, Ben said in a small voice. "There is another aspect I have been giving thought to. There is also the child to be considered. A paper marriage will stop the stigma of illegitimacy; something I am most concerned about. If you throw that into the equation, perhaps a registry office would be sensible?"

Elizabeth stared at Ben; she couldn't believe what she was hearing. Even her soulmate was turning against her. She crumbled into tears.

Over the next two weeks, Ben arranged a registry office ceremony and they both decided that Elizabeth would not say the words obey and would not receive and wear a ring, which is a symbol of ownership like the ones put through the noses of pigs and bulls. She did however decide that she would take Ben's name, but Ben decided that he would take hers also. Therefore, on 12th October 1874, they exited Kensington Registry Office as a legally married couple. No frills, no guests, just a couple of witnesses invited in off the street.

"Mr and Mrs Wolstenholme Elmy at your service," said Ben caustically; she was not amused.

****

The women were in uproar.

"Does she think that this will appease people; that we are simply going to forget that she was living in sin with Ben Elmy? No, no, no! This is not going to go away."

Lydia Becker at the age of 46 years, was formidable and one of Elizabeth's enemies. She was staunchly Christian and saw Elizabeth only as a miserable sinner. She had always been openly hostile to Elizabeth's presence and could hardly bring herself to admit Elizabeth's value to the movement.

Here at this moment, she was moving in to exact God's revenge on this fallen woman. If truth would have it, Lydia owed a lot to Elizabeth, but all she could see was a Secularist with immoral ideals. "I don't believe it anyway. I don't think this sham marriage has even taken place and even if it has it's not legal in the eyes of God."

"She has done such a lot, there wouldn't be a woman's movement without Elizabeth Wolstenholme! How can you take against her like this, she is the heart and soul of the movement" cried a voice from the back of the room. "I predict nothing but bad to come if you take this course of action."

Millicent and her followers looked at each other and remained silent. They felt they had a duty to the movement but their duty to their God was greater.

Millicent Fawcett stood up and spoke to the assembled women. "Let's take a vote. All in favour, raise your hand."

Silence except for the swishing of skirts as arms were raised.

"Against"

Another, much fainter swish of silk.

" Motion passed; Okay, that's it then, Mrs Elmy must go."

And so it was that the women's movement, which she had been instrumental in forming and for which she had slaved so devotedly, turned their backs on Elizabeth in this, her darkest hour.

****

Ben could not believe it. Elizabeth's colleagues, her sisters-in-arms, had turned on her and all because she was pregnant, and it was all his fault. How could women do a thing like this? It was beyond him for sure. How could women be stupid enough to put the ideas of religion; man-made nonsense, before loyalty, love and compassion?

She was broken and he could only stand and watch. Was it not enough for these women that they had broken with their own, sincerely held principles and gone through a civil ceremony in a registry office, a thing most offensive to them, only to have them do this in the end?

Ben was incensed, and Elizabeth heartbroken.

"Lizzy my poor girl, I hope you got seriously angry and told that Fawcett woman exactly what you thought of her?"

"Yes, yes she got the full weight of my wrath, and I told her I resigned, I wasn't going to allow the puffed-up, holier-than-thou, harridan to sack me, Ben."

"Good for you! I would have been very tempted to break my lifelong vow of pacifism and smash a vase over her head. How they have the gall to treat you that way after all you have done and all your devotion. It's terrible and I can't believe it; you started the dratted movement!"

Elizabeth became agitated. "I'm not stopping Ben I shall continue my work as though I'm still employed by the women's movement even if I am not. This is a mistake on their part as I know that they have not got another woman with the knowledge of English Law that I have; they simply have no one that can do my work so it either doesn't get done, putting the cause back years, or I continue to fulfil the role."

And so it was that in the weeks and months that followed, all through the final trimester of her pregnancy, Elizabeth maintained her workload, writing letters and pamphlets without batting an eyelid at the stares and nudges her presence elicited.

CHAPTER 18
The Birth

Elizabeth had had an ache in her back from early morning. It had woken her up at 4:30 am and she had risen and begun her morning chores which she had completed by mid-morning. She had taken a light lunch and sat at her writing desk to work through the afternoon. The backache continued until it began to distract her from her writing.

Lord, I wish this child would come, she thought. I can hardly breathe with the pressure on my lungs; it must be huge by now. She stood to try and get a full lungful of air and in the hope that the movement and change of position would ease the discomfort in her back. She stood by the window looking out across Buxton Road and out across the pasture to the Dane Brook. It was always a soothing and peaceful view and she stood awhile, rubbing her back.

As she turned to go back to her desk the first contraction came. The suddenness and ferocity of it took her breath and she bent double under its onslaught. She couldn't speak for several seconds but as the wave of pain subsided, she called out for assistance.

Sally came running to help. "Has it started Madam?"

When Elizabeth confirmed it had, Sally wrapped Elizabeth's arm around her neck and together, they made their way slowly upstairs to Elizabeth's room where Sally helped her remove her clothes and make her way to the bed. As she sat on the bed it came again. A great wave of agonising pain rendering her speechless and draining the blood from her face. As the pain again subsided, she turned to Sally and grabbing her arm said, "get word to Mr Elmy, I need him here."

"I don't think we need to do that Madam; he'll be back shortly at his normal time. I think we can wait for him but perhaps I should send someone for the doctor?"

Elizabeth looked confused and then as the pain completely retreated, she nodded saying, "Yes, yes, you're right. He'll be home soon, and we will need Dr Davies but be quick Sally I don't want to be here alone."

Sally looked at Elizabeth's face and could see the stark terror in her eyes. She had never seen Elizabeth even remotely frightened. Normally, nothing frightened her, but Sally recognised that Elizabeth was clearly very frightened now.

"Don't worry Madam, I won't be long, this is going to be a long, long night, we're not even started yet. Try to relax and rest between pains."

Elizabeth nodded and Sally disappeared from her view. She heard her leave the house via the front door. She was alone now with her fear. This is it she thought, the hour of my death is approaching. Childbirth took my mother, and I will share the same fate. Everything is stacked against me, my age, my size; I am far too old to survive this ordeal. The next pain hit, and she cried out in pain and fear but as the pain peaked and then died, she spoke aloud to herself. "Come on Elizabeth you know this is nonsense, you don't believe that sort of claptrap. Life has dealt you this card and you are strong, healthy and most of all you are a woman and women do this every day without fuss. Keep calm you can do this."

She heard the front door open as the pain hit again, but this time she was ready. Taking deep breaths, she waited out the pain before turning her attention to the sounds below.

"Hello, where is everyone?" Ben's voice echoed through the hall.

"Here, here Ben" she called and was rewarded by the sound of Ben's hurrying feet on the stairs and relief when his concerned face appeared around the door.

"Dearest, has it started?"

She nodded and the pain came again causing her to wince and suck in her breath. Rushing to her side Ben took her clammy hand "remember what the book said, take deep breaths and try to relax. Count with me one, two, three, that's right, you can do this."

Sally returned to report that the doctor was out on another call, a woman at Mossley was having a hard time birthing twins. A man had been sent with a message. An hour later and the same man knocked on the door of Buxton House.

"Dr Davies says Mrs Elmy will be hours away from delivery so try to relax and he will be with you as soon as possible. Just let things happen."

"As though I could stop them!" cried Elizabeth.

As the hours crawled by the pains became more frequent and more brutal, then at about midnight, the waters broke but little else occurred. By the small hours of the next day, she was so exhausted she slept in the brief respite between pains.

By 10:00 am the next day Ben was beside himself with the horror of it all and cursed long and loud, his voice echoing through the house. "Where is that fucking doctor?"

At 10:30 am Dr Davies finally arrived and hurried to Elizabeth's bedside. He was visibly tired, smelled strongly of drink and was copiously splashed with the blood of his last patient. He hurried forward to examine Elizabeth.

Ben intervened. "Wait a minute! Don't you think you should at least wash your hands?"

The doctor looked at Ben as though he was talking in a foreign language and Ben slowly asked, "Do you know nothing of cross-infection?"

The man looked baffled. "Do you want me to minister to this patient or not?" he asked arrogantly.

Ben looked at him and then weighing up the situation; looked across at Elizabeth who was lying there in her bed, so vulnerable. Should he risk this ignoramus ministering to her, the most precious thing in his life? He went with his instinct.

"No Sir I don't believe I do" was his response, and then he escorted the man from the premises. He turned from the door to find a frightened Sally standing behind him.

"What do we do now Sir?" she said quietly in a terrified but trusting voice.

Ben was also frightened, very frightened, more frightened than he had ever been in his life before. He was in a real pickle now, but instinct told him not to let that so-called doctor loose on his defenceless wife. Right on cue, Elizabeth screamed out her pain above their head.

"Sally, I need your help. Who do the women use? Who helps the Mill Lasses?"

"Mother Hargreaves Sir, she helped my mum with all six of us."

"Then run like the wind and ask her to come and help us."

Grabbing her hat and coat, Sally left the house and ran up Buxton Road.

Returning to the bedroom Ben took Elizabeth's hand, but Elizabeth was somewhere else. She was in a pain-filled house of horror. Her body was pushing and pushing uncontrollably with the pain and now, the pain was not abating at all: it was constant, and it would not stop. She felt like her body was ripping apart as the child was trying to be born; she was surely dying.

Sally returned with Ella Hargreaves who instructed Sally to bring hot water and soap. Scrubbing her hands, she gently examined Elizabeth who was oblivious to the fact, then looking at Ben she said "It is almost here. There doesn't seem to be anything blocking its passage, but I don't need to tell you that this lass is very small and also very tired. The babby is a good size though and not too big; I've seen bigger. Let's get this lass awake and get this babby born."

With that, she shook Elizabeth roughly by the shoulders to wake her and gain her attention. "Come on lass wake up, you've got some work to do. Draw your knees up, come on, look at me lass. I want you to put your heels here on my shoulders, she patted her shoulders, and hold my hands, then when that pushing pain comes pull on my hands and push down with all your strength. Come on wench, let's get this over with."

Elizabeth drew strength from Ella and from the very depths of her body, she pushed and pushed. Another long hour went past but Ella Hargreaves would not let her stop. She was so tired, and the pain was so bad. Finally, the very worst pain of the whole ordeal came, and Elizabeth instead of pushing, drew in a huge lungful of air and prepared to scream.

She never heard the scream because something inexplicable happened. She felt herself leave her body and float up above the bed, in a peaceful and silent bubble. She hovered just a few feet above herself for just a few seconds but at that same moment, the child's head forced itself out of her body tearing tissue in its path and splashing Ella's face with bright red blood. Then she felt herself float gently back down and flop back into her traumatised body. Back to the noise of the bedroom, back to Ella's voice and her ministering hands, but the pain had eased at last; the nightmare was concluding.

"One last tiny little push lass, the head's here we just need to get the shoulders out. Come on, the worst is over, let's get it done."

The pain came again, and Frank Wolstenholme Elmy slithered into the world.

"It's a boy, well-done lass, well-done lass and congratulations Mr Elmy Sir."

Ella was smiling all over her face as she wrapped the baby in a towel and handed him to his torn, battered and exhausted mother. Returning to stare between Elizabeth's legs she said "It's a bit messy down here lass, you've ripped quite badly, but with any luck it should heal well. I did my best for you, but you are such a tiny lass. Ah here comes the afterbirth" and she went to work again.

Ben was stood behind her and had observed the whole ordeal. No, this must never happen again, he could not risk putting her through this another time. Nothing, nothing, absolutely nothing was worth this. Poor Lizzie, my poor, poor girl, he thought.

Elizabeth was oblivious to the afterbirth and Ella's ministration; she was staring at the child in her arms. "Oh, you beautiful thing, you wonderful little boy" then looking up and across to where Ben stood, said "A boy Ben, what shall we call him; Benjamin after his father?"

"No, no, no I rather like Frank; what do you think?"

Elizabeth smiled broadly, "I like that very much."

They fell silent as they looked at their perfect, new-born and then Elizabeth looked deep into Ben's eyes and said "Frank is my delight, but I must never allow him to be my distraction. Back to work tomorrow."

Ella looked up from her work "I'm afraid not Madam, there are things that need to heal down here, you need to have at least 10 days of bed rest. You've not had an easy time of it, you'll need time to regain your strength."

"Then I'll write from here" she responded.

So it was, the afterbirth safely delivered, Elizabeth's wounds tended, and Frank declared fit and healthy with the correct number of fingers and toes, that Elizabeth fell into a deep sleep. Ben sat with his son in his arms. I must think of other ways to share our love. I obviously got the "safe period" all wrong, how stupid of me I was so sure! I can't risk her having to do this again, I could have lost her. Women amaze me, that their bodies can go through this barbarity year after year and yet they survive! He sobbed quietly to himself.

Ella Hargreaves smiled to herself, she'd seen it all before, proud father distressed by the woman's suffering, she'd be needed again next year, it was always the case; human nature and all that.

CHAPTER 19
The Victor

Elizabeth fought hard to regain her strength and vigour, and in the weeks and months following Frank's birth, she established her working pattern. As always work came first and was the first call on her strength and vitality. At first, she found it hard to ignore Frank's cries, but she managed to find a place in her head where she could block him out and not even hear him. Luckily, she had employed a good woman in Sally, and she knew that his every physical need was being attended to. She trusted Sally to be kind and nurturing to her son and so she was able to happily ignore his whimpering.

One of the hardest things that Elizabeth had to do around this time was to go to the women she taught at the Co-op Hall, mostly workers in Ben's Mills and admit that Ben's theory on "safe time" contraception was incorrect. She had taught it to them thoroughly, so they all now knew about the female anatomy and how the reproductive system worked but Ben had not realised that other mammals ovulated differently and that unlike dogs and cats, apes ovulate mid-cycle. It was reasonable to draw that conclusion, but it was a very wrong one. Ben's safe period mid-cycle was actually the exact time when a woman was ovulating and therefore almost guaranteed a pregnancy.

As she stood before her class her legs were weak, not just from the difficult birth she had so recently experienced, but also from her embarrassment. She explained the situation to them and openly admitted the mistake and the fact that this was how Frank had been conceived. A silence fell upon the room as the women took in the information. Many had already deduced that this was the case but had respectfully kept their peace. No one seemed to know how to respond and then a woman tittered and another guffawed and then the whole room dissolved into raucous female laughter.

At first, Elizabeth thought that they were laughing at her but quickly realised they were laughing at the absurdity of the situation. Several others had taken Ben's advice with a similar consequence. However, these women were used to having baby after baby, so to them, it was just an experiment that had gone hilariously wrong; they were not holding her or Ben responsible.

"What's one more when you have a houseful, I gave it a good try" quipped one heavily pregnant woman at the back of the room, and the laughter continued.

"There's worse things than a babby Mrs Elmy," shouted another.

Not from where I'm standing. thought Elizabeth behind her red face, this won't happen to me again, our love transcends the physical act. These women seem to just accept it as their lot in life; one cannot help but admire them.

****

Ben and Elizabeth were working on the Married Women's Property Act, and it took an awfully large part of their day. Writing letters, pamphlets, and speeches to be given at public gatherings in Manchester and London. It was a full-time job and a job that was mentally and physically draining. It took every ounce of Elizabeth's strength and stamina in the weeks after her confinement, but she was resolute and steadfast. Nothing, nothing, absolutely nothing would turn her mind off the campaign for women's rights not even her new-born or her own health. When her body was hurting and weak and her mind was woolly with tiredness she would cover her eyes with her hand, take deep breaths and inwardly chant her mantra: justice, justice, justice.

These were dark days, physically and mentally weak, cut off from her sisters and trying hard to cope with a new baby and all the extra work that brought, Elizabeth needed her mantra to keep her from despair.

However, Elizabeth was too important and too well-known to be off the front line in the fight for justice for very long. The sisterhood soon realised their mistake in dispensing with her services and the loss that was, and she was invited back, an invitation she was never going to refuse.

Elizabeth

I am the victor, but my trophy is heavy. I have been invited back by Mrs Fawcett, but I am finding it difficult to swallow my pride and accept. To find out that the very women I had trusted and counted as sisters, had dispensed so easily with my services because their silly God didn't like my relationship with Ben. Women I fought beside and nurtured, mentored and trained.

Women like Lydia Becker, who actually sent out a deputation to Kensington Registry Office to make sure that the charade of a marriage Ben and I have undertaken, had actually taken place! How dare she! What did she think we did, pretend? The whole thing was a pretence, we had already been married for nearly four years; we didn't need an official piece of paper to tell us that.

Of course, I didn't stop the work, I carried on regardless because I knew that there was only me with the knowledge and ability to do it. Without me, the work would not have been done at all and everything would have fallen under the pressure of it.

Of course, I will accept their offer; I simply have to because the cause is too great and there needs to be justice for women everywhere and truth be told, I need the money, so I will have to put up with the occasional collie-shangles.

Yes Millicent, no Millicent, three bags full Millicent. Your God be with you Millicent. As for Becker, I have no words to show my contempt for that specimen. However, I will smile and accept their false praise and assurances. I'll pretend that I don't know how much they need me and not the other way around. We must have solidarity and unity among the women of the world: something Millicent Fawcett has no concept of. She's far too busy trying to look elegant and well-heeled. Without me and Ben she would be nowhere: yet she sells me up the river for living by my principles, the exact principles she admired me for or said she did; who knows?

Still with Ben beside me and firmly on my side, we can see through their piety and their faithful adherence; we laugh at them behind their silly backs. Onwards and upwards towards the prize, justice, justice, justice.

Elizabeth took up her role in the women's movement again. She had never really stopped campaigning, writing letters and pamphlets and hundreds and hundreds of names on her petitions; to the populace at large, she had never given up her job and was consistently there all the time, pushing forward for women's rights.

Throughout the rest of the 1870s and into the 1880s she campaigned tirelessly for the Married Women's Property Act which allowed women to keep any property that they owned when they married, which was a huge step forward for women's equality, and The Guardianship of Infants act which allowed women to have a say in the upbringing of their children and to have custody if their marriage ended.

The Acts were passed into law in 1882 and 1886 respectively.

CHAPTER 20
Salford Mill

Ben had been arranging lectures and classes for his mill workers for several years and found them to be a receptive and intelligent audience. They had decided they would introduce their students to Secularism, a topic that both Ben and Elizabeth held close to their hearts.

The National Secular Society had been founded in 1866 by their friend Charles Bradlaugh so they invited CB and his partner AB to come to Congleton and carry out a series of lectures at the Town Hall. They accepted and all was in place when Mr Clark the Town Mayor, got word of the fact that the lectures were entitled "No Progress without Heresy" and the topic would be Women's Rights and Secularism and he immediately refused to allow Ben and Elizabeth to hold the events at the Town Hall as advertised.

Ben was enraged but there was very little he could do as the mayor had the backing of the Town Council. There was little use in trying to fight this particular battle as they knew of old that they would be defeated. However, Elizabeth pointed out that there were other venues in the town, so Ben went to his fellow Secularists for help. He was rewarded when Mr Cook of Salford Mill offered the use of his building, so the lectures went ahead.

The events were re-advertised, and the town buzzed with excitement as the date of the first lecture approached. However, Ben and Elizabeth were unaware that the Mayor and the Town Council had dirty deeds planned. They employed a well-known ruffian, a bare-knuckle, prize fighter to recruit a willing mob to attend the lectures and disrupt them.

On the first evening after Ben, Elizabeth, Charles and Annie arrived at Salford Mill, an unruly mob gathered outside chanting loudly and singing hymns. It didn't stop the lecture from going ahead of course, but after the meeting, Ben and Elizabeth had a problem, how to get themselves, Charles and Annie, safely back to Buxton House. The crowd was showing no sign of departing and was getting more and more irate as they chanted and sang outside.

Eventually, Charles took the initiative stating, "I have no fear of this ignorant mob, come on, steel yourselves we are walking out" and with that, he took Annie's hand and followed by Ben and Elizabeth, they bravely walked out of the mill and down Milk Street towards the park.

At first, the crowd stood silently as they walked past but then one of them took up a chorus of "What a Friend We Have in Jesus" and the crowd fell in behind the group. On reaching the park the mob began to pelt them with stones and as they passed through the gates a large stone struck Elizabeth above her right eye. Blood gushed from a large cut, and she screamed in shock and pain.

Charles was incensed, he stopped dead in his tracks and as Ben and Annie helped a dazed Elizabeth through the park gates he shouted, "Just see, just see what you have done, the Police will be here shortly, let's see what they have to say."

The crowd quickly sobered up and realised they had gone too far and slowly the marching and singing faded as they silently slipped away one by one across the fairground.

On gaining Buxton House, they examined Elizabeth's eye and realised it was a really deep cut, so the doctor was sent for, and her wound stitched and dressed. It quickly healed but it left a deep scar both on her face and in her heart. She hated violence and yet it kept coming up in her life in ways over which she had no control.

The following night, sporting her dressing, Elizabeth and her group attended the second lecture. This time the dissenters had managed to gain entrance and were inside the hall itself. The prize-fighter was very vocal and challenged Charles to a fight and Charles, being no shrinking violet, accepted the challenge and leaping from the platform into the crowd, promptly set about the man.

Charles won the fight and escorted the villain from the premises. Most of his followers left with him but they remained outside the building chanting hymns and throwing stones. One stone broke a window and hit Annie on the head, but the lecture went on and the good people of Congleton heard what Annie had to say about Women's Rights and the plight of women under English Law.

All in all, the lectures were a great success and went down in history as two of the most interesting and notorious events Congleton has ever seen.

Elizabeth

What a night, what a disgusting night! These people live in ignorance and seem to have no desire to learn new ways or challenge the teachings of old. So narrow-minded, so willing to just toe the line and allow things to stay just as they are. No free thinking, no acceptance of what science has taught us. They amaze me! As long as they have a smoke and a pint of ale, they are happy. They care not about the plight of their poor women and as for the women themselves, some of them are as bad as the men. They will not fight back or campaign for the vote, they appear happy with the way things are, they know no better I suppose.

Only yesterday at Eaton Mill, I heard the most brutal conversation between two of the mill lasses. Joan was advocating for the vote and stating quite correctly that it is a fundamental democratic right for all citizens not just men, but Maud was saying she cared little about politics and was happy to do whatever her father told her. I almost joined in the conversation to talk her out of her mindset, but Joan was doing so well I left them to it.

Joan didn't win Maud over, she was the type of closed mind you could never win, and she resorted to insults calling poor Joan "a man in women's clothing" and suggesting that she was a sapphist. It is a sure sign that they are losing the argument when they resort to that sort of thing.

I felt pity for Joan, but she was used to it and had all her answers ready, but Maud laughed and walked away to the other end of the cutting bench just as I expected. Well done Joan I thought, we can only win the war one person at a time, and you may not have won this one, but you have chinked her armour.

CHAPTER 21
A Meeting of Importance

The familiarity of Manchester her hometown, meant that Elizabeth paid little attention to her surroundings: unlike Ben who always looked around, taking in the smells sights and sounds from the moment he left the train.

"Walk or cab?" Ben asked.

It was a typical Manchester day, dark and overcast with heavy clouds which looked as though they were about to shower the populace with the infamous Manchester rain. Mancunians were of course used to this, they understood that their great city was only in existence because of the damp climate, which was so beneficial for the lucrative cotton industry, earning it its nickname Cottonopolis: the irony was not lost on them.

"Let's walk; it's only a cock-stride and we could do with the exercise," Elizabeth answered with a grin, and taking Ben's arm, they stepped out. As they passed the carriage rank, she raised her skirt to avoid the copious amounts of horse manure that littered the road, as they progressed down Piccadilly.

They were on their way to stay with their good friend Richard Pankhurst a fellow Socialist and fighter in the cause of women's emancipation. He was a middle-aged lawyer who had become firm friends with Ben many years previously in his time teaching in Manchester and now they worked closely together on the Married Women's Property Act and the vote via several, high-profile organisations based in the city.

Richard had recently surprised Ben by suddenly marrying a much younger woman and that was where they were heading now, to meet the young bride. The Elmys were amongst the first people to be introduced to her and they were intrigued as to what kind of woman Emmeline was to capture his heart so late in life. She must be someone really special Ben thought; he had always considered that Richard Pankhurst, despite his commitment to female emancipation, was a committed bachelor.

A half-hour stroll through the city centre, which remained thankfully rain free, brought them to their destination, a large elaborate house, the home of Richard Pankhurst and his new wife Emmeline.

The door was opened by a butler in full livery who stared down his nose at them. Ben was not in the least intimidated and Elizabeth was used to such treatment, because of her gender and small stature; men in particular made the mistake of thinking her weak in both body and intellect. Ben pointedly stepped over the threshold removing his hat as he did so and passed it theatrically to the supercilious manservant.

"Mr and Mrs Wolstenholme Elmy; we are expected I believe."

Elizabeth smothered a smile and walked in behind him, she knew that Ben had no time for that sort of thing and was making a show for her benefit.

"Ben, Elizabeth welcome my friends, welcome." Richard came from the parlour with a huge smile on his face. Married life was obviously suiting him thought Elizabeth.

"Please leave your bag in the hall, Clarkson will take it to your room, come and take tea, Emmeline will be down in a minute."

He led them into the drawing room. It had been completely redecorated. It was now bright and festooned with fresh flowers and lacy antimacassars and doilies; a complete change from the rather dark, old-fashioned, bachelor room they were used to seeing. Elizabeth stood and looked around delightedly.

"Oh, how lovely Richard"

Richard looked a little embarrassed. "I am so glad you approve Elizabeth; I think that Emmeline has a very, feminine taste and I rather felt it was a little over-the-top, but as I had promised her a free hand with a complete redecoration, I could hardly say no."

"No, no Richard, it is delightful, what say you Ben?"

"Oh yes indeed, very pleasant."

Elizabeth heard a sound in the corner and her attention was drawn to a small wicker cage hanging by a chain from the ceiling. She moved across the room to get a better look and was appalled to find a small linnet imprisoned inside it. The cage was so tiny that the poor bird could hardly spread his wings but still, he tilted back his tiny head and chirped out a distressed song. Elizabeth's heart went out to the poor bird. At that moment the door opened and a tall, well dressed young woman entered the room. Elizabeth looked her quickly up and down and smiled warmly.

"Emmeline, darling, may I introduce to you two of my dearest friends, Ben and Elizabeth Wolstenholme Elmy: Ben, Elizabeth, I give you my wife Emmeline."

There was a slight beat and then Emmeline walked forward with her hand outstretched. "Mr Elmy Sir, Mrs Elmy" she smiled broadly.

"Oh, Ben please, no formalities" taking her hand in his Ben raised it gallantly to his lips. She smiled courteously then turned to Elizabeth and as she shook hands with her.

"I have been so looking forward to meeting you, I hold you and your work in great esteem. I see you have been admiring my newest acquisition, Toby, my linnet?"

"Yes I have, he is very pretty, but don't you think it rather cruel to keep a bird in so small a cage?"

She looked Emmeline in the eye and Emmeline was silent for a split second, then any response was cut off by the arrival of the tea and they sat to partake of it as the threatened rain finally arrived beating mercilessly on the windowpane.

Elizabeth's remark about Toby had caused a slight atmosphere but the bird was not mentioned again; the moment passed, although not for Elizabeth who was painfully aware of the tiny creature and his plight for the remainder of their visit.

Thus began one of the strangest friendships that Elizabeth was ever to have. Two strong women with bold ideas and the bravery to carry out the work, but with some fundamental differences of opinion: what could possibly go wrong?

The following weeks and months saw these two strong, committed women working closely together. They were like-minded on most things and Elizabeth took Emmeline under her wing and they planned their strategy for getting the vote. They very quickly forged a strong bond with Emmeline standing in awe of the tiny firebrand and pouring over Elizabeth's writings.

However, there were some contrasting and fundamental differences in their attitudes and beliefs. For Emmeline, a devote Christian, Ben and Elizabeth's secularism did not sit easily nor did their committed opposition to marriage, their pacifism and their commitment to animal welfare and the fight against vivisection.

For Elizabeth, Emmeline's sense of entitlement and her preoccupation with her looks and her wardrobe rankled as she considered such things as trivia and time-wasting nonsense.

Elizabeth was also very aware that Emmeline considered her to be lower-class and inferior. Thus, she never felt fully accepted by her.

Elizabeth

Well, what an interesting young woman, who would have thought an old goat like Richard Pankhurst could have captured the heart of such an intelligent person, and captured she most definitely is. One can see she loves him dearly and he is obviously in love with her. It is nice to see, and I think she is bright and I believe wholly committed to the cause.

What a change in that dark, dull house too. So many lacy bits and pieces; so feminine and pretty pretty; but oh, that poor little bird, sitting there on his perch inside that tiny cage. He has a water pot and a bowl of seed, but he can hardly stretch his little wings. I could not hold back; I told her the cage was far too small for his needs, but she insisted he sang so was therefore happy. Her sense of entitlement really gets to me; how can she be so blind to the suffering of that poor bird?

Emmeline

My word what a strange woman. So tiny, so ill-kempt! Her clothes are so worn and old-fashioned. Her hairstyle is like something out of an ancient magazine but her brain, her intellect more than makes up for the dishevelled look. She has something that I want, brain-power and amazing knowledge. I must befriend her and make sure that we stay on right side. I would not have even been in the same room as those two if Richard had not insisted I meet them, and now I am over the shock, I can see why he wanted it so much.

I need to look past the lack of finesse and breeding to see the intellectual woman beneath; but oh, the fuss about my bird Toby! Of course, it's not cruel, he wouldn't sing if he was unhappy, would he? I have a catch though, their lack of commitment to the Christian faith and their rejection of God. One must always mistrust atheists as they are most assuredly in league with Satan.

****

The parlour at the Pankhurst home was filled with women, it was one of Emmeline's regular "at homes." Elizabeth was distracted as usual by the sight and sound of poor Toby, still imprisoned in his tiny elaborate cage, still singing his distressed song for the entertainment of Emmeline. Elizabeth was almost as distressed as he was and she actually longed to enter the room and find the cage empty, his death was the only thing that was going to stop his suffering, for Emmeline refused to listen to any reason on the topic.

Emmeline was proving to be rather spoilt, as people with money and status so often are. She had an ingrained perception that all her wealth and entitlement was ordained by God and her Bible told her that God gave man dominion over all living things, so she considered animals a commodity to be used and abused as she saw fit. Never considering the pain and suffering she inflicted on them; Elizabeth and Ben's anti-vivisection campaigns were of no interest to her.

For Elizabeth, Toby was a beautiful living creature that needed to live in his element out in the wild. His capture and incarceration in that disgusting cage was something that gave Elizabeth discomfort and a feeling of hopelessness. She longed to free him as she had Theodore as a child.

She had of course, spoken to Emmeline about her cruelty many times, but Emmeline had insisted the bird was well looked after. Sadly, it was one of several things that she was unable to get Emmeline to see the light on. Emmeline's flagrant disrespect for animals was something that Elizabeth found extremely distasteful. The hats she wore with the huge bird feathers as decoration, and the fur coats and wraps were all gained through the death of beautiful, sentient beings but she openly laughed when Elizabeth pointed it out to her.

Elizabeth's pacifism and belief in the sanctity of all life were also causing a deep rift in their relationship. She sighed and moved away from the tiny cage to take a seat with the other ladies who were drinking tea and waiting for the meeting to begin properly.

"Order sisters, order" said Emmeline rattling her spoon against her teacup,

"Mrs Elmy has something to say about the Guardianship of Infants Act. Over to you Elizabeth dear."

Elizabeth prepared to speak.

CHAPTER 22
Frank Wolstenholme Elmy

Frank

This is one of my earliest memories.

Tick-tock, tick-tock, the large clock on the wall is marking out the time. I am lying on the window seat the warm sun shining through the window and onto my motionless body. Tick-tock, tick-tock, goes the clock and thump-thump, thump-thump, goes my head. Every movement causes searing pain through my ears and through my head with a sound like the weir on the River Dane in Congleton Park, the crashing deafening sound of water. It makes my eyes go funny and I see two clocks and two mothers.

Not surprisingly I am reluctant to move any part of my body because of the pain it engenders. The only parts of my body I can move without extreme discomfort are my eyeballs. I'm staring across the room in the direction of my mother who is working away studiously at her writing desk. I will her to look up and notice my predicament, see my pain, give me comfort, acknowledge my presence but she is concentrating, and I know better than to disturb her when she is working. Her work is very important, the most important thing in the world and I must wait until she breaks off.

I watch her rise from her desk and scurry across the room to the bookcase, take down a large tome, carry it back to the desk and rifle through it until she finds the page she wants and then write quickly onto her paper. Tick-tock, tick-tock, thump-thump, thump-thump; another hour passes and still I am ignored.

Presently, Sally enters the room carrying a tray containing tea and sandwiches. Placing the tray down on the desk, she turns to me and says, "come on little man, let's be having you."

The words die on her lips and her face registers concern. She hurries across the room to my side, places a cool hand on my forehead and cries "oh! Frank you're not well, are you little man? Madam, Frank is poorly, he has a temperature, and his face is badly swollen, I think he needs the doctor."

Mother looks in my direction and pays attention at last. "Oh dear, see to it will you Sally" and then returns to her work.

As Sally gently lifts me into her arms the pain sears through my head and ears with the accompanying roaring sound, like the sea at high tide and I cry out in pain and misery.

"There, there dear, let's get you into bed," she says, as she carries me from my mother's hallowed presence.

Sally is kind, she ministers to my needs, calls the doctor, gives me aspirin, and helps me to drink some water. She holds my head as I am sick into a bowl, wipes my fevered brow and makes me feel a little better.

I am three years old and what three-year-old does not want the love and comfort of his mother at a time like this? I don't want Sally I want my mother. Tears creep from my eyes and slide down my hot face. Sally wipes them away as I fall down, down, down into a deep sleep thinking only of my mother.

It's not that Elizabeth didn't care about Frank, it's just that she simply could not spare the time from her work to attend to his needs. Frank was her absolute delight, but she would not allow him to be a distraction. She trusted Sally to attend to Frank's needs and that was how it had to be.

Later that day the Doctor diagnosed Frank with mumps, a painful but short-lived childhood disease. He lay in bed for a week longing for his mother's hugs but never received any as he was asleep when she finished her tasks for the day and looked in on him.

This was the way of life for young Frank Wolstenholme Elmy, he was a sensitive child but was not treated with any sensitivity by his parents as they were both far too busy with their many campaigns. He was not ill-treated, but neither was he allowed a childhood. Both parents treated him like a small adult, and he spent great expanses of time alone. Treated as an outcast by the other children, he was friendless at school. insular and alone.

As he grew into a slightly built young man he was perceived as effeminate by his peers and most gave him a wide berth as someone who was different and therefore a target. Frank learned to like his own company, but he was also deeply, deeply resentful.

CHAPTER 23
The Years Roll On

As the years rolled on through the 1880s, Richard Pankhurst, Ben and Elizabeth were rewarded with the Married Women's Property Act passing through Parliament and the Guardianship of Infants Act following swiftly in its wake. The repeal of the Contagious Diseases Act completed Elizabeth's hat-trick and they were delighted. However, these campaigns had taken a toll on their meagre finances.

On one particular day, in the late 1880's, a day that stood out for Frank Elmy for its rarity, he had been allowed to accompany his parents to Manchester on a visit to the Pankhursts no less. He disliked the noise and the crowds of the city and the Pankhurst's house with all its finery felt strange and unwelcoming, but it wasn't the remembrance of the house, that stayed with him, it was his mother's doting on Christabel and Sylvia. He watched her interaction with them and the obvious love in her eyes and was consumed with jealousy.

He deduced from her manner that he as a boy, was somehow inferior to them. The journey back to Congleton was all talk of the amazing Pankhurst sisters and how clever and accomplished they were at such a young age. His father said they were truly destined for great things. Frank sat in silence absorbing what was being said and it registered with him that he was somehow inferior to those young girls and that he was a disappointment to his parents. He felt it deeply, but it was just one of many perceived injustices that he carried in his heart.

Elizabeth
What beautiful children Richard and Emmeline Pankhurst have produced. Christabel is an absolute delight. I love spending time with her. Clever, articulate and questioning, just the sort of daughter I would have loved. Richard asked Ben and I to be Godparents when she was born. Richard held a high regard for his old friend Ben, but we declined and said, we would not be any good at the job as we're not rich and don't believe in God. Richard looked disappointed, Emmeline relieved: she makes no effort to show her disapproval of us and our secular lifestyle. Bah hoo Emmeline your small-mindedness does you no credit. I fear for those girls, they are already smothered in their mother's relentless Christianity. I can only hope that they will question and see through the

the mire and one day achieve their freedom.

****

Although the Elmy's experienced great success through the 1880, on a personal level their finances were not doing well. The collapse of the silk industry hit their mills hard and they found it more and more difficult to keep producing their silk crepe in the face of cheap foreign products imported from abroad.

There were weeks when it was impossible to employ the number of factory hands they needed and both Elizabeth and Ben regularly worked shifts at their mills to keep them running.

These dark days were exhausting for Elizabeth. Rising in the early hours, she carried out her household duties, washing, cleaning and preparing the meals for the day and then working beside the mill lasses for a 12-hour shift. Returning in the early evening she cooked the evening meal and then began her letter writing which took her into the early hours.

No household servants now, it was down to her to carry the weight of the family home, her campaigning and help keep the mills open, no easy task.

Frank

The sound of female laughter cuts through my head like a knife. What do they keep finding to laugh at? Silly, silly women; they grate on my nerves.

None of them are in the least bit aware that I am sitting here, nose in a ledger "doing the books." Why would they; I am nothing to them, so my presence is ignored. They prattle on and on, constantly giggling and they say nothing of any interest; nothing remotely sensible; nothing of any value, that I can see anyway.

When "she" walks in their voices change and they become more serious, hanging on her every word as though she is some great messiah. My mother, the great matriarch, goddess; queen of all she surveys. Utterly ridiculous!

Even she ignores me. Frank Elmy – part of the furniture; the silent, fly on the wall; seeing all, hearing all: not one of them has an ounce of respect or thanks for me.

Just look at her over there: Annie Coppock. I know she has a violent husband; I know he kicked her down the stairs last week. Saw her limping back and forth along the cutting table and heard her tell her friend in hushed whispers. She was totally oblivious to the fact that I was sitting here working, taking it all in. Do they think I am deaf?

God, I hate women, I hate their raucous stupidity. If I was Annie's husband, I would make sure I kicked her harder next time: shut her up for good. This world would be a better place if such women were eliminated once and for all.

****

Annie Coppock was listening intently for the sound of Charlie's return. She had arrived home from work tired and stiff from a 12-hour shift at Albion Mill. She had hoped that Charlie would have been home, made a fire and supervised the children. Ah the children, that ever-growing band.

How she had loved Annabelle her first, however, when John arrived a year later, she was a little overwhelmed. Two babies in two years, a full-time job and a husband who demanded she wait on him hand and foot. The housework quickly took a back seat as her workload increased and her strength diminished.

Three years later and two more children making four under 5 years old. By now the love had disappeared and all that remained was worry, hard work and fear. Fear of losing her job, fear of more babies and mostly fear of angering Charlie.

Of course, she had the memories of that sweet, brief time when she was in her teens and Charlie had been her ever-attentive beau. What happened to that gentle boy who wooed and won her heart? She couldn't remember when the rot set in, and he changed into a demanding, violent tyrant who treated her with the utmost contempt.

She remembered the first slap: it had taken her by surprise, and she hadn't known what to do or think. She had been holding Annabelle in her arms. She'd just been feeding her by the fire. He hadn't come in from work on time so the meal she had prepared was still in the oven, now dry and ruined. He had come in worse for drink and had loomed over her demanding his meal.

"Wait a minute Charlie, Annabelle needs her feed" she had said

His hand had started to slap her around the ears again and again. She had cradled Annabelle's head to protect her, and the terrified baby had screamed out her fear. Charlie had attempted to take the child from her arms, pulling her roughly but Annie had fallen to her knees and wrapped her body around her daughter to protect her, placing her hand to protect the baby's head. The man had rained slap after slap around her head and when his anger was finally spent, he had flopped into an armchair and told her to get in the kitchen and make him some food. She had little choice but to go to the kitchen and try to make a meal with her screaming daughter in her arms.

When he had finished his meal and Annie had managed to calm and feed her terrified child, he had demanded his "conjugal rights."

Of course, the next day he was shame-faced and repentant. Begging her forgiveness and assuring her that it would never happen again but pointing out that it was she who had caused the incident; she provoked him with her insubordinate attitude; if she only behaved herself and did as she was told there wouldn't be a problem.

He had played gently with Annabelle on the hearthrug, cutting the picture of the perfect, loving husband, but Annie was no fool she knew that it would happen again. She knew of men who beat their wives and children; they didn't change but rather grew worse with the passing years. As she expected that incident established the pattern for her married life. One battering after another, one child after another, one 12-hour shift after another.

She often wondered what it was she had actually done to deserve her life. She was still under 30 years old and had given birth 8 times. Two stillbirths, a cot death and five living children. By now she was praying that Charlie would die, that some horrible accident would occur at his workplace, or that he would stumble under a cart's wheels on his drunken walk home from the pub. It was her perception that such a happening was the only thing that would release her from the misery that was her life.

There were times when she saw glimpses of the old Charlie shy, loving and kind, but most times, he was angry and sullen and when he was in drink, she just prayed for her and her children's safety. There was no help for a woman like Annie or her children, there were far too many Annies in the world.

This particular day she was at the cutting table walking in pain back and forth. It had been bad last night, probably one of the worst times. He had actually attempted to force her up the stairs, but the babies were downstairs, hungry and needing attention. She had tried to stand up to him, something her friends had told her she should do, but this incited him to even greater anger. He had loomed over her on the stairs and then suddenly kicked out catching her on the thigh and causing her to tumble down the last four stairs twisting her back as she went.

She was desperate now and had told her overlooker Bridget O'Day, who had enquired into the reason for her condition. The dam had burst. She had suddenly opened up and let it all come out and Bridget had been understanding.

"We must tell Mrs Elmy; she will know what to do." Bridget said.

"No, no I don't want people to know, they will think bad of me."

"Annie, do you think people don't know already? Walls are thin in these terrace houses. This man is going to kill you and what will happen to your poor children then? Be sensible we must ask for help. I honestly can't live with your secret, if anything happens to you or those kiddies, I will never forgive myself. Your husband is a monster who doesn't deserve you; I must tell someone, and I can think of none better than Elizabeth Elmy. I am going to Mrs Elmy, and you should come with me."

So, she had reluctantly agreed, and Bridget and Annie had gone quietly to Elizabeth.

Annie's tale of woe was no surprise to Elizabeth, she had heard many such stories and through her work on the repeal of the Contagious Diseases Act and her work with the mill lasses, she was well acquainted with men like Charles Coppock.

"Annie, we must get you and your children away. Are you prepared to leave this man? Are you prepared to move to another part of the country and take your children with you? If you are then I can arrange a job and a helping hand with accommodation to help you get settled. Are you ready to take that step?"

"I don't know, I don't know, I never realised such a thing was possible. Won't the Police bring me back?"

"No, so long as you have help and a job there is nothing they can do. If you do not break any law, they should never find you. Things are different now; the laws have changed, and you have rights you never had before. My friend moves in the right circles, she is beyond reproach; she has all the power that money and rank bring. Take a few days Annie, think about it and meanwhile, I will make enquiries. My contacts know where best to relocate you and your long-suffering children."

Annie broke down into tears and looked pitiful.

****

On a dull day in April Elizabeth, Annie and her children boarded the train for Manchester and at Piccadilly Station, they changed trains for Rochdale in Lancashire where their train was met by a group of women who took the tired children and their terrified mother to a place of safety, gave them a hot meal, a warm bath and a clean, fresh bed.

Annie Coppock and her children were successfully relocated to Rochdale and safety. Annie got work in a local cotton mill and the women set her up in a small, terraced house. Thanks to Ben, Elizabeth and their dear friend Josephine Butler, one family was set free from the tyranny of domestic violence.

Only Ben and Elizabeth knew Annie's whereabouts, even Bridget was kept in the dark although she had a good idea what had happened and who was responsible the day Annie Coppock failed to attend work for her expected shift and Elizabeth stood in her place working her shift on the cutting floor, keeping quiet whilst the rumours were flying around the mill via the "tea-talkers" that Annie Coppock had done a flit.

The following day Charles Coppock came to the mill gates demanding to speak to his wife and was most put out when he was told she wasn't there. Bridget had looked smug when she saw him through the mill window walking dejectedly away.

"That's put a stop to your little game, my lad" she had said aloud to herself, or at least she thought it was to herself, but she was overheard. In this office the walls have ears, or at least Frank Elmy did.

Elizabeth

You don't know how pleased I am to have got Annie Coppock away and safe. You don't know how many women are in a sorry state like her and are too frightened to make the break. They fear many things, destitution, their abusive partner finding them and the contempt of their friends and family: in their fear and weakness, their thinking is skewed, and they find it impossible to think outside their fear.

So many times, I have made similar arrangements for a mill woman only to have her return to the abusive brute and resume her life of misery. They remind me so much of my father's dog Theodore; even though they are given the chance of freedom they still return to their misery and chains. Like Teddy of old, it's the only thing they know, and they return willingly to their miserable lives, mistaking the brutal bullying for love, and thinking it's the only thing they can expect; it is heart-breaking.

Regardless, we press on for justice for women everywhere, even if it is they who so often mindlessly work against us. It is so hard to see them so accepting of the ways of the patriarchy and adopting so completely the mindset they are required to have. We fight against some strongly embedded customs and practices that need to be broken.

Meanwhile, we fight on. Justice, justice, justice.

CHAPTER 24
Treachery and Revenge

Ben and Elizabeth were in the drawing room at Buxton House. They had been deep in conversation for some time and the topic was their son Frank. He had recently received his final exam results and they were very pleased and proud to see he had passed all with flying colours, but there were deep problems.

Frank's future had not been considered in their fight for justice, they had been so single-minded in its pursuit that they had overspent their meagre resources. Today that fact had caught up with them and they were feeling, not a little embarrassed and cowed.

They accepted that Frank had been an exemplary worker and scholar, finishing the school day and then going to the mill office to keep the books on two evenings a week and all day on Saturday. He didn't complain and always had his head in a book. As Frank entered the room, he was uncharacteristically bouncy, excited and smiling widely.

"Well, what do you think? I'm hoping to take up my offered place at Cambridge and Uncle Joseph has said I can lodge with him and Aunt Therese."

He was greeted with silence and the broad smile slipped slowly from his face as a suspicion crossed his mind. "Well, come on, say something. I was hoping that you would be proud and happy for me. I wasn't expecting this, why the silence?"

Ben and Elizabeth exchanged sheepish looks and then finally Ben was forced to speak. "Frank, we are indeed very proud of you, but I am so sorry, we just haven't got the financial resources to pay university fees and your keep. In fact, in all honesty, we can hardly keep the mills open and a roof over our heads. The collapse of the silk trade and the money we have spent on the Married Women's Property, and the Guardianship of Infants campaigns has all but cleaned out our coffers; we are perilously close to bankruptcy. I'm sorry son it's simply not possible."

"You must be jesting! You cannot have spent everything on your bloody women, I don't believe it. Had you never considered what I wanted in life?

Did you think that I wanted to spend my days book-keeping in that wretched mill?"

Anger was pulsating through his head in a series of waves. He lifted his hands and covered his ears to try and drown out the thunderous noise, but he had lost control. All his hopes and dreams of getting away from this ridiculous town and his selfish, heartless parents were dashed. All his hard work in school, studying for the entrance exam, all in tatters before his eyes.

He dropped his hands and rushed forward towards his mother, he towered over her menacingly, but Elizabeth was unafraid, she had faced violence so many times, that she felt she could easily manage her own son's outburst of rage.

"You mother of all people, you know what it's like to be denied an education. How can you do this to me?"

True to form she stood her ground and stared back at him sternly. "It isn't about you or me Frank. This is about justice for women and girls. You have the means to continue your education just the way that I had. This house is full of books, avail yourself of the education at your fingertips and stop with the self-pity."

Hearing her words, he turned and ran from the house, slamming the heavy front door in his wake.

"Oh dear!" then looking at Ben she continued, "He'll get over it, it's not the end of the world. Still, it is a pity I suppose."

Ben stared long at the solid door his son had just passed through, then dropping his head he answered. "Yes, I suppose you're right, you usually are. It's still a great pity though, that we couldn't offer our son more."

****

Frank

God, I was angry, self-pity indeed. I had been denied everything even my mother's love and all for the sake of women. There is always a crowd of them hanging around, complaining all the time, asking for handouts and help. Beaten wives, forsaken lovers, destitute prostitutes you name it, they get my parent's full attention as long as they are female. Women and their issues; I was incandescent with rage. She would have moved heaven and earth to get me to university if I had been her daughter. That has been my only crime; I was born the wrong sex.

All the rejection of my childhood, it had been locked in for too long, it just came spilling over. My parents just don't give a damn. I can't go home, not yet anyway, I have to calm down and bury this gross injustice deep in that secret place where I have stored all the hurt and hatred of my life. I have harboured it for years, all the hurt, rejection and indignity of being Frank Wolstenholme Elmy.

Revenge is a dish best served cold and I shall eat my fill. I have a secret plan, a plan I have been devising for years. It started as a game when I was about nine or ten but over the years it has become more and more elaborate, and I have covered every eventuality.

In the beginning, it was not serious, it was just a way to pass the lonely hours while waiting for my parents to come home. However, of late it has become an obsession and a possible way of getting even. I am well-practiced at sneaking about unseen, that's my life, quietly hanging around in the shadows. I see all but no one sees me. It is the perfect revenge; it will hit them right where it hurts, and no one will suspect me at all.

****

A week later, in the small hours of Sunday morning, Frank left the back of Buxton House and walked quickly down Queens Street. At the bottom he turned right into Havannah Street and from there he made his way down to cross the Dane at the little footbridge. He had been planning this a long time and now here he was standing in the darkness. He could hear the thundering water of the Dane and see the black looming shape of Eaton Mill, his father's pride and joy. This is the place where he toiled for hours on end, week in week out, year after year, surrounded by the women he despised so much.

The town was silent, the pubs closed, the late-night revellers long gone home; he had chosen his time well. He made his way through the familiar front gates of the mill yard and then, using the shadows to hide himself, he made his way to the rear of the building. Letting himself quietly in through the small rear door, he climbed the short flight of wooden stairs that led to the office, his familiar abode.

He went from there into the huge working area where the silent looms stood, menacingly in the moonlight. He knew where he was going and made his way there through the darkness. So familiar was this place to him that he needed no light to miss the obstacles in his way, he knew exactly where they were, and he could have passed through with his eyes closed.

These objects were the symbols of his imprisonment; the chains and instruments of torture that kept him anchored to this miserable place. He had nearly escaped but his escape route had been denied him by his selfish, loveless parents and he was poisonous with intent.

His final destination was a small storeroom at the side of the building. Piled high with rolls of silk cloth and the floor strewn with off-cuts, it was the ideal place to wreak his revenge. He poured a small jar of paraffin oil onto the cloth and stepped back to consider his work. Just a small spark and there will be no stopping this.

Frank spoke aloud "Mother, Father I have had enough of you. Vengeance is mine."

And with that, Frank Wolstenholme Elmy struck a match and threw it onto the pile of cloths he had previously soaked with the paraffin. They ignited immediately and he watched for a minute or two to make sure the fire was well lit and then quickly left the building.

Instead of leaving by the same route via the mill gates, he left by the rear and crossed the fields executing a large loop into Town Wood and then dropped down through the park and home to Buxton House, where he went silently to his room to avoid waking his parents.

Two hours later Elizabeth and Ben were awakened by noises in Buxton Road, Fire bells ringing and people shouting. As Elizabeth came awake, she realised that Ben was already dressing and then came the sound of pounding on the front door. Elizabeth rose and Ben, now fully dressed, ran from the room and down the stairs to the front door. She followed him to the landing and stood in her nightdress listening to the conversation below.

"Mr Elmy Sir, Eaton Mill is aflame."

She turned and ran into one of the back bedrooms and looked through the window. Sure enough, she could see a strange orange light in the sky above their precious mill. Frank came out of his bedroom pretending to rub the sleep from his eyes. "What is it Mother?" he asked innocently.

Ignoring him she ran back to the landing as Ben closed the front door and ran out into the night. She turned back and looked at Frank's questioning face.

"Frank, I fear we are in serious trouble, Eaton Mill is on fire."

****

All was lost. The mill was badly damaged, and the insurance was insufficient to cover the repairs needed. With a heavy heart, Ben put the mill up for sale to clear his many debts.

In reality, all three Elmy Mills needed to be sold and after the sale, there followed a prolonged battle to keep their heads above water financially. The fire and the campaigns for equality had taken a heavy toll. In total despair, Elizabeth declared that she had had enough and decided to retire from the women's movement and work in general; she was tired and weary.

They were thankfully able to retain the ownership of Buxton House, but it was heavily mortgaged and the sale of the three mills barely covered the debts incurred in the fight for The Married Women's Property Act and The Guardianship of Infants Act.

Elizabeth and Ben settled down for what they hoped would be a long and happy retirement. However, the Universe had another plan for Elizabeth Wolstenholme Elmy, she wasn't finished yet: there was still work to do in the fight for that longed for justice.

PART THREE

Fame and Notoriety
1890 - 1918

CHAPTER 25
Clitheroe Lancashire
February 1890

Imagine if you will a wild, windy day in late February 1890. The place is Clitheroe in Lancashire. A small sleepy mill town where nothing exciting ever happens, especially on a Sunday morning like today. The Parish Church bells are tolling to mark the end of Matins, the sound is carried away and across the open countryside on the blustery morning wind.

Let us stand awhile and observe the scene.

Our heroine Emily Jackson, is saying goodbye to the vicar in the church porch. Bear with me as we watch her walk slowly down the church path, stand still at the halfway point, and look up into the wild sky inhaling deeply. A sudden gust buffets against her, flapping her coat and threatening to dislodge her large elaborate hat.

Can you see her turn her back to the wind and lift her elegant, gloved hand to hold the hat in place, laughing slightly as she does? Watch her as she glides slowly along the church drive towards the lych-gate but as she passes through the portal her attention is attracted by a sudden movement to her right. She is grabbed roughly, and a large male hand is placed over her mouth to silence her screams.

Emily recognises her assailant immediately; it is her estranged husband, Edmund. She knows his touch and knows his strength. Her legs are grabbed by a second man, one she does not recognise and between them, they lift her from the ground and carry her the short distance to a waiting carriage and then bundle her inside.

"Drive on" Edmund shouts to his driver and away they go into the distance and into history.

This whole occurrence is over so quickly and witnessed only by Emily's sister and the vicar who are still making small talk at the church door and being attracted by the scuffle, have turned to see the awful crime enacted.

Mrs Edmund Jackson has gone to her fate little knowing that she is about to become, for a time, the most famous woman in England and her abduction will change the law for English women forever.

****

Buxton House

Elizabeth had been seated at her writing desk for the last two hours and it was still only 9:00 am. She had been working on a few letters and her autobiography. She has more time on her hands these days but cannot break the old habits. Rising at dawn, preparing the family meals for the day, cleaning and washing and then breakfast for herself, Ben and Frank. These habits were ingrained and not easily discarded, and the call of her writing desk was still as strong as ever.

She had regained her strength considerably since her retirement and was finding that having time on her hands was not something she found enjoyable in any way. She knew that there was injustice in the world; she knew that she had pledged to fight for women and girls and frankly, she was beginning to feel guilty. There was so much still to do and here she was languishing in Congleton doing precious little.

She looked up towards the window and saw the paperboy pass, turn, and climb the steps to the front door. Then she heard the clink of the letterbox and the dull thud of the newspaper landing on the doormat. Next, she heard Ben's footsteps cross the hall and then the almost inaudible groan, as he bent double to pick it up: he was feeling his age. She listened as his footsteps retreated to the kitchen.

About a quarter hour later Ben hurried down the hall and into the drawing room where she was at work. He walked over to her desk and dropped the paper before her saying "You must read this Elizabeth" and he pointed his finger at the front-page headlines.

"CLITHEROE ABDUCTION CASE"

Elizabeth gave it her full attention and slowly read the report. When she had finished, she lifted her head and looked intently at Ben.

"This encapsulates everything I have ever fought against; this is couverture in all its awful glory. That poor woman is being held against her will. Look, just look at the court report, look what Jackson said."

> "I therefore took my wife, and have since detained her in my house, using no more force or restraint than was necessary to take her and keep her."

She stared wide-eyed at Ben. "He is openly admitting rape, and the judge has done nothing to stop him."

Ben responded. "In fact, he has given him carte blanche, he has even been given police protection whilst he does it. We have to do something Elizabeth, YOU have to do something" he looked at her in earnest.

She waited a few moments to think clearly and then she said, "We are going to Clitheroe."

As it happened, they went to Blackburn for it turned out that that was where Edmund Jackson's house was and where poor Emily was being held, and the scene was unbelievable. Elizabeth simply couldn't believe her eyes. There was Emily's sister, father and uncles, camped out before the house of Edmund Jackson. They knew that Emily was inside being held captive and being forcefully treated and they wanted her released forthwith so they could take her home to safety. Jackson was not relinquishing hold of her anytime soon and the police were in attendance to make sure that Emily, his legal property, stayed right where he wanted her to be.

A huge number of supporters were also there, some with tents and camping equipment; they had pledged support to Emily's family and were intending to stay until she was released. The newspaper reporters from both national and local newspapers were also there, watching the proceedings with a voracious interest.

I can't believe that this is possible, thought Elizabeth. The police are here to protect a rapist, protect him from Emily's family, a family that love her and want her safe and well. They are helping him to hold this poor woman prisoner: this is everything that is wrong with the law in this country. I must prepare a good case to appeal this Judge's awful decision.

"The original case had favoured Edmund Jackson: the judge had stated that the law of England was quite clear: a man's wife was his property; a woman pledged before God to honour and obey her husband and therefore agreed to the situation," Elizabeth said to Ben and Frank back at Buxton House.

"Under English Law, a man has full possession of his wife's body and can demand his conjugal rights at any time and in fact, he can beat her if she refuses; just so long as the stick is no thicker than his little finger!" replied Ben.

Frank was silent as usual, but his mind was swimming with foul thoughts. Bravo I would say, bring it on, I hope Edmund Jackson wins this case and this ridiculous appeal is thrown out of court. Why can't she keep her nose out of things?

"Frank dearest, the coal man is just pulling up at the front, can you attend to him for me?" Frank rose silently and left the room to attend to Mr Anders the coal man.

"How do Frank, how's yer Ma?" Ken Anders asked. "I see she's in the papers again. By eck lad, she doesn't half get about, dunt she?"

Frank smiled and nodded but kept his counsel. He stood and watched Ken as he lifted the filthy sacks of coal from the cart and carried them round the back, depositing their contents into the coal cellar.

The bodies of the working men had always fascinated him, much more so than those of the women. He found the rippling muscles strangely attractive; whilst the females repulsed and disgusted him. He counted seven sacks and then handed the coal man his money.

"Thanks Frank, see you next week" called Ken as he climbed back onto his cart. "Gerrup" he said, flicked the reins and the tired old horse, took the strain, and moved off up Buxton Road.

****

Elizabeth worked tirelessly to prepare her case. Corresponding regularly with Emily's family and on the day of the hearing she travelled to the Court of Appeal with Ben at her side.

The court was packed with Emily's family, lawyers, women activists, news reporters and curious members of the public. As Elizabeth was called and entered the dock, her legs were like jelly, but as she climbed onto the steps her mantra was ringing through her head, justice, justice, justice, and all nervousness disappeared as she opened her mouth to speak.

> "In Elizabethan England, there was a common saying "the air of England is too pure for a slave to breathe in" yet it was not until nearly 200 years later in the r eign of George III that it was finally established in law that as soon as aslave sets foot on English soil, he is a free man and able to own property and is covered and protected by English Law.
>
> From the date of that judgement, the right of every human being to personal freedom has never been in question, except in the case of every English wife. Every married woman in England is the property of her husband: however brutal a tyrant she may, unfortunately, be chained to – though s he may know he hates her, though it may be his daily pleasure to torment her, and though she may feel it impossible not to loathe him – he can claim from her and enforce the lowest degradation of a human being, that of being made the instrument of an animal function contrary to her inclinations."

When she finished the assembled were silent, only the frenzied scratching of the pencils of the press could be heard and the footsteps of the tiny woman who had rendered them speechless. The court rose as the Judge went to deliberate.

"Break for lunch, which means we get a two-hour break and then he comes back to give a speech and announce the decision. Most people seem to be remaining in the court; afraid of losing their seats I suppose. There is a large crowd outside that would love a seat in here. We would be wise to remain I think Elizabeth; I did instruct Frank to bring us refreshments, but he hasn't made an appearance. Do you think something could have happened?" Ben looked worried.

"No, it's typical of Frank, he will have forgotten. You know what he's like Ben. I did bring some refreshments but there will be no hot drink. He'll be off somewhere looking at buildings, I should think; pass my bag from under the seat please Ben."

Two hours later the court reconvened awaiting the judge's return. Finally, he entered in all his finery and commenced his deliberations. Elizabeth and Ben listened with bated breath as the judge droned on and on until finally, he overturned the first decision and declared that Mrs Jackson should be released from her husband's home forthwith.

Ben whooped for joy and lifted Elizabeth in a bear hug, the court erupted with cheers and not a few boos, but they were unmoved by that: they were fully in the ecstasy of the moment.

"Elizabeth, darling you did it!" shouted Ben.

"Yes, yes, yes, that's it, couverture is gone, married women are as free as married men to have control over their own bodies. What a red-letter day; justice has been done."

Elizabeth was overjoyed at the hard-won piece of justice.

Mrs Emily Jackson was reluctantly released by her husband and taken home by her delighted family. She was later granted a divorce, citing his cruelty.

Decent people were scandalized that a woman like Elizabeth should talk about such things and a group of "God-fearing" men objected to the appeal court's decision. Bishop Roberts headed an attempt to take the case to the House of Lords, but he was unsuccessful.

Elizabeth
It is truly wonderful when hard work and determination pays off and we see progress being made. A fine and happy day; victory and justice; the Universe be praised!

"The clear and decisive declaration in the Clitheroe Case of the legal right of a wife to her personal freedom has made further amendments to the law more easily and speedily possible."

Elizabeth Wolstenholme Elmy 1891

CHAPTER 26
The Women's Emancipation Union

Back in harness Elizabeth is fighting as always, against the patriarchy and the class structure for the rights of women and girls. Recharged and revitalised by her success in the Clitheroe Judgment and using her many contacts she founded yet another women's organisation, the Women's Emancipation Union.

Elizabeth had been working with Richard and Emmeline Pankhurst in the Women's Franchise League, but the two women never really hit it off. Elizabeth perceived that Emmeline looked down on her lowly state and she felt the disadvantage of not having the buffer of a large personal fortune.

Although Emmeline and Elizabeth had a deep respect for each other's work, Emmeline's staunch Christian faith and Elizabeth's free and open atheism meant they often crossed swords on their fundamental differences. Although Emmeline easily conceded to Elizabeth's greater intellect on most things, she had that ingrained state of mind that came from accepting religion without question. This infuriated Elizabeth as it was the basis of her own life to always question everything and thoroughly think things through.

Elizabeth considered Emmeline's fixed mind very odd as Emmeline was so obviously a free thinker in other areas; sadly, she seemed unable to get through the rigid teachings of a staunch, Christian childhood. There were many times when Elizabeth's quiet patience was tested to the full.

"What are you hatching up now old girl?" Ben asked.

It had been evident for some time that she was finding the constant conflict with Emmeline tiresome, and her nimble brain was thinking of a new campaign.

"I've been thinking of asking Mrs Russel Carpenter to join me in founding a women's union. She is very active in the fight for equality and more importantly, she has a large fortune. If I could persuade her to bankroll the endeavour, then we could make a considerable difference and further our campaign for the vote."

"Oh, so what of the Women's Franchise League? I know you share my frustration working with Emmeline and Richard, but what would be the aims of this "women's union" and how would it differ?"

"They are too stifled by their attitudes to religion and class structure. It means that wonderful, intelligent, working-class women cannot find a foothold in the organisation; it is so wrong and much talent is being lost. I have gone as far as I possibly can with my support; there is only so much one can turn a blind eye to. I fear it has reached the end of the road and I shall resign anyway; Emmeline has become intolerably puffed up with her own pride.

I would like to focus on four specific things and state them at the outset so that I can turn away all the old arguments from the religious upper-class controllers. I shall write to Mrs Carpenter and state my aims and see if she will meet with me to discuss my campaign in detail. We have met before many times, and I perceive her to be a like-minded and dedicated woman. Fingers-crossed I am reading her correctly Ben, I feel she could be our salvation."

"But what are the aims? You must tell me then I can advise; or am I to be kept completely in the dark for all time?" he asked crossly.

Elizabeth looked faintly amused; she knew Ben was pretending to be hurt in order to entertain her. There was no way she was not going to tell Ben every detail of the organisation she had in mind; she knew that without his quiet and steadfast support, things would be much more difficult for her. He was her rock and her strength. She sighed a fake sigh and rolled her eyes.

"Its points will be rights with men in all matters affecting service to the community and the state; opportunity for self-development through education; freedom in the choice of career; equality in marriage and parental rights." She glanced across at him and he was smiling broadly.

"Bravo Elizabeth, and have you found any enthusiasm among your sisters? Do you think that there is a serious opening, indeed a need, for such a venture? I agree that it all hangs on the patronage of Mrs Carpenter or some other wealthy personage, it is no small undertaking and will need a huge bank roll and we are not affiliated with any political party so have not got access to their coffers. We would need a benefactor with deep pockets."

"I believe so Ben, and of course, that great "muck-raker" William Stead is anxious to take up the cause. I have been discussing it with him ever since the success of the Clitheroe Judgment; he was as delighted as we were with that outcome. The case seems to have touched a nerve with some Christian women too and at long last it has made them sit up and realise just how the law is wrong and how controlling the Church is. Some are even questioning the authority of the Bible. At last, they are beginning to see that the vote is just one part of women gaining freedom and equality.

I simply cannot continue working with Emmeline and Richard, I have reached the end of my tether, and I must go on, so I am resolved to approach Mrs Carpenter; I shall write this very afternoon."

Elizabeth met with Mrs Carpenter and found it was not too difficult to win her over to the campaign. She was well aware of Elizabeth's huge reputation and trusted her completely. If anyone was going to pull this off it would be Elizabeth Wolstenholme Elmy, she thought. And so it was that the Women's Emancipation Union was founded in September 1891. It was financed by donations from its supporters and members and enjoyed the sponsorship of Mrs Russell Carpenter.

Throughout the 1890s Elizabeth was writing on average 300 letters a day, all by hand. From her little house in Congleton, she established a worldwide movement, and ran a slick and disciplined business that influenced not only England and Great Britain but countries as far afield as the USA, South Africa and New Zealand.

In the background Ben was also working, perfecting his pamphlets, first used at Moody Hall, into books on sex, childbirth and family planning. The WEU published these first sex education manuals. The Human Flower in 1894 and Baby Buds in 1895, which were aimed at children and which Ben wrote under the pseudonym Ellis Ethelmer. For adults, he wrote Woman Free in 1893, Life to Woman in 1896 and Phases of Love: As it Is As it May Be in 1897.

Elizabeth's work with the WEU pioneered some crucial cross-class and cross-party collaborations, encouraged women's resistance to authority and advocated making Women's Suffrage a test question in the selection of parliamentary candidates.

By 1897 Elizabeth, Ben and the WEU had been working on a new female suffrage bill. They had been working with Ferdinand Beggs MP, who was a nephew of Emily Faithful, a loyal friend and member of the WEU. They felt sure that this time Beggs's Bill would pass and would bring the much fought for vote.

However, their opponents in Parliament were not going to allow the bill to pass and once again the Elmys and the women of England were dealt a terrible blow when the bill was thrown out of parliament; time wasters used up the precious time with pointless debate.

The women were in despair, and it was generally perceived that this was the end of the line, that the vote would never be won and that the women had been well and truly defeated this time.

The subscriptions to the WEU halved almost overnight and then when their great benefactor Mrs Carpenter suddenly died, it was the fatal blow and the WEU was forced to disband in 1899.

Elizabeth despaired yet again; she knew that without money all was lost. She had no fortune and no political party to back her work from their coffers; the WEU was virtually bankrupt, so she had to hold a final meeting and disband the Union.

She feared that she would never see the justice she so craved.

Elizabeth
The final meeting couldn't help but be a sad affair, but the women were kind to me, thanking me for all my work and holding me up in great esteem. Women coming from as far away as the USA to sing my praises, trying to turn the event into a celebration instead of a wake. This isn't what I work for of course, but it is nice to be appreciated even though I am a total failure. I feel like I have let everyone down. All the years of hard work, all the writing, all my many sleepless hours and all for nothing.

The women are scattering. My strong band of stalwarts are drifting away in defeat. Oh, how those smug men must be crowing over their brandies tonight; they have well and truly defeated us this time.

Is this the end? No, no, no I cannot allow it.

Justice, justice, justice: onwards and upwards.

CHAPTER 27
The Boer War

War Against War in South Africa

Sad last year of a dying century,
That dawnest in the stress of storm and strife,
Of witless waste of sacred human life,
And the wild pomp of War made revelry.
Dost thou but bring a message of despair?
Have heroes wrought, have martyrs died in vain?
Is there no healing for the deadly pain
Of greed, and lust and Hate and sickening Care?
Not so, this fateful hour of Destiny
Calls each who seeks, and hopes, and strives for Good
To higher effort, to a loftier mood,
To nobler life; so may the holy Three,
Love, Truth and Justice, rule from shore to shore,
And peace make glad this earth for evermore.
Elizabeth Wolstenholme Elmy - 29th December 1899

"It looks like that's it then Ben, we are at war in South Africa again." Elizabeth's face was a picture of distress. They were sitting at the breakfast table in Buxton House, and she had the Manchester Guardian open before her.

"Have they no shame? All that loss of life again and all for gold." Ben responded. "We keep on writing letters, protesting, pointing out the senselessness of it all, but it is pearls before swine. There seems to be this massive desire for war: the jingoism and flag waving, is there no one with an ounce of sense?"

They are sharing the table with their dear friend and fellow campaigner William Stead. His face was also a picture of despair as they spoke. A well-known journalist and writer William had been changing the face of journalism with his many investigative campaigns. He shared the Elmy's commitment to pacifism and had been campaigning with them long and hard to try to prevent a second Boer War, but they were now looking at the prospect of another long war in Africa, and they were bereft.

William was also a radical campaigner for women's rights and took a particular interest in women who were caught up in the thriving sex trade in the City of London. He had fallen foul of the law and his enemies in high places, when he became involved with the infamous Eliza Armstrong Case, when he contrived with a reformed procuress to buy a young thirteen-year-old girl from her drunken mother for just £5. He hadn't, of course, put the young girl in any danger, indeed she was taken by Bramwell Booth of the Salvation Army to France and a place of safety, but the powers that be and the courts decided he was guilty of an offence, and he was sentenced to six months hard labour.

"They are saying all the usual things; "it will all be over by Christmas" whilst any fool can see we are in for a long and bitter war. They are masquerading the cause as Englishmen not being able to vote in South Africa, but in reality, it's all about control of the Rand Gold Fields, they don't fool me or anyone else who takes the time to read up on the history, it is all so very predictable. Working men and boys will give their lives so that rich men will get richer. That paper is full of Kruger-spoofs, there's hardly a true word in any of the reports." William was flicking a disgusted finger at the Guardian lying before Elizabeth as he spoke.

"Twas ever thus. How they have the cheek to go to war because Englishmen are unable to vote in South Africa when every English woman is denied the vote here in England; it is maddening," said Elizabeth.

"Indeed dear" said Ben, "All we can do is stick at it, protest, write, write and write again. At least you have your new typing machine, which will surely speed up your letter writing."

"Yes, I am forever grateful to the Wilde Family for their kindness; such an expensive gift." She looked towards her writing desk where the new machine sat. It had caused such a commotion in Congleton when it arrived; people were walking past her window trying to catch a glimpse of the expensive, new-fangled invention as she worked at learning how to use it with any speed. In the end, she opened the window and allowed them a better look in order to get them to leave her alone. It had caused her such merriment.

There wasn't much merriment in the room today though. It was a very gloomy place full of defeat and despair. The very worst of their fears had been realised.

"I think you have a good attack line there Elizabeth, you can make a point about that fact and press home the need for female enfranchisement. Grab the attention for the cause whilst they are busy flag waving and burying their dead." William said earnestly.

Elizabeth and Ben nodded in agreement both their faces displaying the deep emotion they were feeling. They were more than aware of what was coming, and their hearts were filled with dread.

The following week Congleton sent six young men off to the war with great fanfare. A band played as they marched to the train and a happy, smiling, flag-waving crowd saw them off from the station. Ben and Elizabeth were horrified and yet resigned to the conflagration ahead.

And so began another long campaign in the face of horrible news coming in from Africa, both official and unofficial by way of her many contacts. Ladysmith, Mafeking and a "Scorched Earth Policy" so horrible that Elizabeth wept over the letters she received from her South African contacts. Concentration Camps, starving women and children; she lost sleep over their plight. Letter after letter, speech after speech and all to no avail. She needed her mantra through those dark days. Justice, justice, justice.

****

The winter of 1900 was particularly cold in Congleton. The snow fell heavily, and February was bitterly cold with deep snowfalls. Ben was ill for the whole winter and spent seven long weeks in bed. Buxton House was like the Arctic and the Elmys picked up several frozen Robins in their garden.

"The poor birds must be really suffering" said Elizabeth who was suffering herself. The striking cold caused Elizabeth's rheumatism to be extremely painful and she had open chilblains on both her hands and her feet. Getting warm and staying warm was a constant problem; their lack of funds meant that coal had to be rationed and Harriet's frequent gifts of food were gratefully received.

The Elmys longed for Spring.

1901 arrived and still, the war raged on in Africa and Elizabeth, writing to the Manchester Guardian said *"We need to educate people so that they can hope. It is not through antagonism and warmongering that a nation can improve itself. I think we have enough grief right now as evidence of that."*

At long last the "witless waste of sacred human life" ended on 31st May 1902.

Armistice Day

The whole of England was celebrating, and Congleton was no different. There were marching bands and great revelry, feasts and much merriment, but not in Buxton House. Ben, Elizabeth and Frank were inside with the shutters up.

"Quite a benjo" said Ben in disgust.

Not for the first time they were at odds with the populace and the citizens of Congleton. They refused to celebrate thinking only of the terrible loss of life, not just the men and boys that had left the town for this travesty of a war, but the lives of the other troops and the women and children that had starved in the Concentration Camps.

They knew that the good people of Congleton were ill-informed and had their strong nationalistic feelings ratcheted up by the propaganda and desire of the ruling classes, whose heads and hearts were firmly in their bank accounts.

They knew that there was many a kitchen in Congleton that contained a broken-hearted woman, crying for a lost husband, son or brother. A woman who had no say in the proceedings: no vote, no voice. They gave the most precious thing of all, their children, fathers, husbands and brothers; Elizabeth saw the situation as typical of all she fought against.

The Elmys had made posters and stuck them on the outside of the windows and committed to staying inside in protest for the whole day.

"I doubt they will even notice," said Ben.

"I care not; at least I will have my voice heard, even if it is just a mere whisper." Elizabeth's eyes were red from crying.

As the day wore on into the evening, they could hear the boisterous crowd getting drunker and drunker until by nightfall, the noise of their drunken revels came wafting up from the park behind their home. A bonfire was lit, and their singing was heard until the early hours of the next morning.

"It is agony for us Ben, but imagine what it must be like for those who have lost loved ones; are they expected to celebrate too?"

"Be of good heart Elizabeth, we cannot win them all, but at least you have been vocal and have attempted to get the point across. History will tell who stood on the right side and who lined their own pockets at the expense of sacred human life.

Now we must put this sad episode behind us, re-group and press on. We have the vote in our sights and Balfour looks set for office, we need to plan our strategy.

Justice, justice, justice.

CHAPTER 28
Women's Social Political Union
1903

"You have all asked and asked for the vote time and time again, well I for one intend to get it! It is more than time we stopped merely asking the patriarchy and start demanding! It is long overdue, it's time for action, real action! We need to take up arms and start doing instead of talking!"

Christabel Pankhurst, now a fiery young woman, was addressing a group of women in the parlour of the family home in Nelson Street Manchester. It had become their home after the untimely death of Richard five years earlier. He had left considerable debts which had necessitated the move to a less salubrious abode.

"I agree Christabel, we have waited long, far too long. What do you suggest?" Elizabeth was enjoying the energy in the room. She adored the Pankhurst girls and saw much of herself in Christabel and Sylvia, she understood their thinking and shared their passion.

"Direct action of course! Actually, doing something! Deeds not mere words!"

"What kind of deeds? I have been gathering names on petitions for years; they are always ignored. I have formed committees and societies, written and lobbied MPs and community leaders all to no avail; they simply bat us aside. What do you suggest, for I will surely join you and put my shoulder to the wheel, for I as much, if not more than any of you desire to see justice. I have been fighting since I was 12 years old, and we are still no nearer the vote than when I started. If you think there is something else, that I can do then I beg you, tell me please!"

The Pankhursts fell silent and looked at Elizabeth. Now 70 years old she was still a firebrand of energy, and her brainpower was undiminished. Her heart was still the heart of a fighter, and she was ready and willing to help, and they knew it. They also knew what they owed this tiny warrior.

"I suggest as a start that we form a women only political party with a single agenda – female suffrage! We will be very visible and very active gaining attention by a series of high-profile stunts." Christabel declared.

"What kind of stunts?" Elizabeth asked.

"Well, I did hear of a woman in America who disrupts local politicians when they are campaigning. Turns up at their hustings with a loud hailer and shouts over them as they try to give speeches. She is very effective in gaining attention for her cause."

"I like the sound of that Christabel, that could gain lots of attention not always the right sort; but that never bothered me. What of this new party then? Should it not be a union? You know I have always steered clear of political parties."

"But we need to be political Mrs Elmy, can you not see that? If we are to gain the vote and social justice, then we need to unashamedly embrace Socialist principles." Elizabeth looked at the earnest face of Sylvia.

"I agree but it opens up a whole new area for attackers to twist the subject away from female suffrage and onto other subjects. Because of your father's open and honest membership and his campaigning with the Independent Labour Party we will be seen as the female arm of Mr Hardie's party."

"Then how about we call ourselves the Women's Social and Political Union?" Emmeline looked around to see what affect her suggestion had gained and was rewarded to see her daughters smiling in agreement. Elizabeth however, had narrowed her eyes and was obviously thinking it through. "Elizabeth dear?"

"I still foresee problems and I feel sure that the Liberals and the Tories will take the view that we are the Labour Party but if we are intending to be more politically active then I can think of no better name."

With Elizabeth's, somewhat guarded agreement the WSPU was officially formed in October 1903 with Elizabeth sitting proudly on the executive whilst holding deep misgivings in her heart. She liked the idea of Deeds not Words, the motto they decided on, but was worried about the young hot heads; she feared they could get out of control.

CHAPTER 29
Treacherous Men and Richard 1
1906

Elizabeth, Emmeline and their sisters were excited. They were upstairs in the gallery above the House of Commons, that group of campaigning women, led by Elizabeth who had spent so many hours lobbying MPs, writing letters, gathering thousands upon thousands of names on so many petitions. There was an air of quiet confidence and the feeling that today, this time was going to be the culmination of all their hard work.

"This is an exciting day, I feel sure it will be our red-letter day, a day of glorious triumph; this bill must pass. We have worked hard on its writing and carefully nurtured its passage through the house. This is the third and final reading: today is the day" she told them.

"Shhhhhh" said a voice and the Right Honourable MP for Peterborough rose to speak.

"My honourable friends, on my way to the house today I passed a bright shiny, brand-new motorcar. It was amazing to see it sitting there in all its glory. I decided there and then that I would like to own such a machine and made up my mind to enquire about the price of such a vehicle at my earliest convenience. It was so new and innovative that I ...."

Half an hour later he was still talking, refusing to give way, and ignoring all attempts to silence him. Eventually, after a further half hour, he gave way to the MP for Maidenhead.

"Gentleman, I put it to you that man cannot live by bread alone and that is why I have decided that I will be purchasing a herd of animals so that I can make sandwiches and therefore eat more than just bread. I may even make some cheese and butter from the milk they produce thus having cheese sandwiches also."

The women stared at Elizabeth in disbelief. "What's happening Elizabeth?"

"They are talking it out, filibustering and there is nothing we can do. They will keep on and on in this manner until the time allotted for the debate has run out. It will then be cast into the dustbin and never heard again. It is the same old tactic and is quite within the rules: all is lost, our bill will be thrown out again."

They stayed there for a further three hours until the bill was declared out of time and thrown onto the Parliamentary scrap heap. Yet another bitter disappointment.

The women were incensed. A woman shouted something from the gallery and the MPs looked up and sniggered. It was like a red rag to a bull and the women's anger overflowed. They poured from the gallery, down the stone steps and out into the courtyard their feet echoing in the huge hallway. Some were screaming in anger, some were crying, some were simply stunned into numbed silence.

Elizabeth began to address them, but the police came and tried to move them on, but Emmeline shouted, "this way sisters" and led them towards the statue of Richard the Lionheart.

Elizabeth was suddenly enthused with super-human strength, and she rushed forward towards the statue and called to Emmeline "Quick help me up."

Emmeline quickly hoisted her lightweight sister upwards and grabbing the horse's leg, Elizabeth pulled herself up onto the plinth. Gaining her balance, she turned and surveyed the sight before her. The women were being joined by a crowd of others who had been outside. They were pouring into the square, a rushing river, a torrent of anger. She lifted a hand and as they fell silent, she began to speak.

> "Sisters this is not a good day. This is a day of deep betrayal, a day of anger and despair. You are right to feel anger, I too feel that emotion, it's burning deep, deep within my soul.
>
> It is righteous anger; justified anger, for we have been b etrayed and humiliated. Yes, yes be angry sisters but do not feel despair, do not allow it to consume you. We may be down now and yes; we may have been defeated but this is not the end, we will not be stopped. This is just another door that has

> been slammed in our faces; one of many, but it will not stop us, we will prevail. We will knock again and again and again until that door finally opens to us for good."
>
> "Sisters we need hope, in the place of despair. We need truth instead of the lies and trickery. We will use our magical, peaceful powers to achieve it. Powers of hope, and truth and love. With these three mighty weapons we will vanquish the barbarity in a peaceful and loving way.
>
> I call upon you, do not retaliate in kind! Stand in peace and love."

The women cheered and shouted encouragement and from her lofty height on the statue, she could see the police rushing towards the gates: she knew that within seconds those uniformed thugs would rush into the courtyard and start arresting her sisters.

She looked at them a confused, emotional and angry group. She knew she must keep that anger boiling but she needed to defuse the present situation somewhat. She could not condone action that would endanger life. She could see that there was the potential for violence and violence was never good; she had to think quickly.

She pointed towards the huge building and continued.

> "Those men in there might have won this battle but they will not win the war. We will fight on because we have right on our side and we have the prize before our eyes, they have won today by stealth, lies and corruption but we will win by honesty, peace and love.
>
> Do not retaliate, do not resort to violence and hatred. Keep calm and we will see the glorious day when we will have justice, justice, justice."

Elizabeth watched as the police rushed through the gates with truncheons in their hands. She saw them make straight for the better-known women, grabbing them roughly and almost carrying them to the gate and the Black Maria. She saw two policemen grab and hold a young girl and watched in horror as her breasts were fondled and one lifted her off the ground whilst the other tried to put his hand up her skirt as they carried her away. She shouted to the men. "Unhand her Sir; I see you"

One turned and laughed saying. "Just checking she's not a man. You never know with you lot."

She continued to watch as the riot police behaved in this disgusting manner towards her sisters. It was mayhem and the police left her where she was. She was sure that eventually she would be arrested like her sisters and awaited her fate but when most of the women had left, many arrested, many making a hasty getaway, she was still there standing on the plinth, a pathetic figure. Emmeline had been one of the first arrested and taken away the rest had scattered in panic.

A policeman looked towards her and shouted, "Get down you stupid old woman; thank your lucky stars you're too old for prison." With those words, he left.

A group of MPs had gathered at the front of the building to watch the spectacle and they were laughing without restraint as the Black Maria left with the women inside.

Her oldest friends Alice and Harriet eventually returned and helped her down and it was a disgruntled and unhappy group that made their way from the Houses of Parliament that day. Elizabeth felt old and defeated.

Frank
Oh Lord, just look at this newspaper, whatever next? She is 74 years old and climbing onto statues making a complete and utter fool of herself. Would that she had fallen from that lofty height and killed herself. Will there ever be an end to this?

Why can't she just accept that women are never going to get the vote and that is that? At least she's getting paid for it now. That stipend from the women's movement, along with my meagre wages from Buglawton

District Council is keeping our heads above water financially. We can still pay the mortgage and keep a roof over our heads and put food on the table.

What would she do if I decided to marry? She hasn't even thought of that or thrown it into the equation? She would never consider my life important. Not that marriage is very likely: I could never marry, women disgust me. Why would I saddle myself with a millstone like that? No, I'm waiting for the inevitable, I will gain my full inheritance and get my own little piece of justice.

CHAPTER 30
Ben's Death 1907

Frank

My father is ill again. I can hardly remember a time when he wasn't an invalid, weak heart, bronchitis, but I can see him deteriorating on a daily basis now. She is very attentive; notices every cough and every ounce of weight he loses.

See Mother dear, it is possible to work on your campaigns and give time to a loved one too. More evidence of her great indifference to me. No love lost here Elizabeth: the feeling is mutual. I need to get my act together or I will lose out yet again. If he leaves all his worldly goods to her, she will surely spend it on the campaign for the vote. I will never get a look in.

I have to admit burning Eaton Mill was not my most intelligent endeavour, there will be scarce little to inherit.

****

Elizabeth is on the train going to London; she has an important meeting to attend with a group of MPs about a new bill that is being prepared; but her thoughts are back home in Buxton House with Ben, he has had a hacking cough for many weeks, and he is losing weight rapidly. Last night he finally admitted that he was coughing blood. She knew what that meant, tuberculosis: the great killer of the working class, the scourge of the age.

She knew that it meant almost certain death or at least a long-protracted hospital stay and that it was very contagious. Oh, Ben darling, whatever am I to do without you? She had been pushing that terrible thought away from her mind for several weeks but now it must be faced.

When she returned to Buglawton in three days' time, she would take control and demand that he consult a doctor; because it was obvious that Ben was going to soldier on regardless until he dropped in harness.

Again, as so often happens, fate took a hand and Ben took ill at a council meeting whilst she was in London, and it was Frank who called out the doctor. By the time she returned on her allotted train, Frank was waiting with the trap and a face that was ashen and strained.

"Mother, Father is ill and it's not good news."

It was like a blow to the solar plexus. "What is it Frank, just tell me; is it TB?"

"No mother, even worse, cancer of the lung."

"Oh, Christ no!" She reeled with the shock. "How long has he got?"

"Mere weeks; the doctor said it has spread extensively."

"Does he know? Has he been told?"

"No, not told but I think he may have guessed. I was waiting for you; will you tell him Mother?"

She went quiet as she briefly considered the situation. She knew that the medical profession advised against telling patients that their ailment was terminal, but as always, she had her own opinion.

"Yes, yes I will tell him, he has the right to know exactly what we know, I shall not try to keep it from him."

"Will you continue with your campaign?"

"Yes, we are at a crucial stage. Campbell-Bannerman the new Prime Minister, appears to be on our side, this could be the breakthrough we've been waiting for. Justice Frank, justice. I'd like your father to see it before he goes."

Frank turned away in disgust. He had his own plans; he needed to rake back some of the money he felt he'd been denied. He would look after his dear departing father, but his will needs looking at, he thought. He would get it out and look at it at the first possible opportunity. He would not be cut out of what little was left of the Elmy monies. He could outwit his mother quite easily as she didn't suspect him capable of foul play, but he was, oh yes, he was, as she would learn.

Elizabeth hurried through the door of Buxton House and straight upstairs to where Ben lay.

"Darling Ben" she cried as she rushed to his side and cradled his emaciated body in her arms.

"Elizabeth, please don't distress yourself. I know what's wrong with me. I have easily deduced the truth from the doctor's face and from the reaction of Frank after the doctor left. I had suspected TB but it's cancer, isn't it? "

There was a beat and then he continued "tell me the truth dearest, for to offer false hope is pointless and cruel and I know you are neither of those two things."

Elizabeth looked deep into the eyes of the man she loved more than life itself. They were sunken into his fleshless face, and she was struggling to control her emotions and find suitable words. Then, regaining her composure, she slowly nodded.

"Yes, yes my darling, I fear we must part" and with that, she sank her head onto his shoulder and wept uncontrollably.

The following week Frank Elmy visited their solicitor to enquire about the will and found that his father had left everything to Elizabeth, just as he feared. However, over the next few weeks he put it to his parents that they had considerable debts, which was true, and if Ben left everything to Elizabeth those debts would pass to her as his lawful wife and that would probably render her homeless and bankrupt.

No, it would be much better if Ben changed the will and left everything to Frank, that way the debt would die with Ben and of course, dutiful loving Frank would always take care of his beloved mother.

So it was that a new will was drawn up and signed by Ben, making Frank Wolstenholme Elmy the sole beneficiary of Benjamin John Elmy's estate.

****

Ben fought on valiantly as Elizabeth worked hard with the new Liberal Government to draw up a bill to give women the vote.

Campbell-Bannerman promised them much and Elizabeth worked tirelessly, leaving her very sick husband at times when she wanted only to be with him. Ben himself equally dedicated to his work, was translating Tennyson's "The Princess" into his beloved Esperanto, and he stubbornly worked on to its completion.

As March 1907 came in "like a lion" Buxton House was a place of quiet expectation. Elizabeth sat by Ben's bedside throughout Friday the 1st of March, listening to the wind howling round the chimney pots. She remained there throughout the night and through Saturday moving very little and leaving him only for the necessities, but by late evening she was tired to her bones and Frank suggested she take a nap on his bed, and he would take over the vigil.

In the small hours of Sunday 3rd March, Frank woke her to say his Father was failing fast. She rushed to him but by now Ben had lost the ability to speak, but the gleam in his eye showed her that he recognised her and as she gathered him to her and placed a warm kiss on his dry lips, Benjamin John Elmy left this world leaving Elizabeth alone and distraught.

She was comforted by her belief that although his body was dead, he had been reunited with the constant life of the Universe, returning to the stars from whence he came.

Elizabeth

Can one die of a broken heart? My darling Ben has gone before my very eyes. What am I to do without my rock and my strength? How can I face this world without him? I am hopelessly alone. I truly feel like my pain is terminal. Oh, Ben my love what am I to do?

CHAPTER 31
Life Without Ben

A Robin was singing in a Springtime tree: early morning at Buxton House. Elizabeth stopped to listen with a heavy heart. How is she supposed to continue, how can she go on? From where will she draw the strength? The mainstay of her life, the rudder and driving force, was gone; cut so cruelly away leaving her so very alone.

The funeral had been well attended with many fine eulogies and readings of his poems. Their dear friend William Stead read "The Princess" in Esperanto; he would have been delighted she felt sure, but now it was all over, and she didn't know which way to turn.

She walked out into the garden to better hear the tiny bird. Ben had loved birds, and the tenacious little robin was one of his favourites. She saw him at the end of a branch of the oak tree, the rising sun behind him casting a yellow light.

"Oh beautiful, darling bird" she whispered.

The dark branch and the robin's red breast stood out against the pink, yellow of the morning sky and filled her with a feeling of peace.

"Come on old girl" she heard Ben's voice in her head, "Come on, pull yourself together, you cannot give up now. The women of England need justice, remember your mantra."

She sat down on the garden bench and watched the little bird until he took flight and swooped away.

He's gone, he's gone. I wish I could die or fly away myself; leave it all behind, but I cannot. The job isn't done yet, I have to gather my strength and I have to move forward.

Justice, justice, justice."

****

London

The women were excited. They had a meeting scheduled with the new Prime Minister, Campbell-Bannerman. Elizabeth had written the bill and knew it was sound and within the law, as the law now stood. They needed the Prime Minister to support the reading of the bill. They had gathered thousands of names on a petition, and they felt that this time finally, they would be listened to and treated fairly.

They were crowded into the meeting room at number 10 Downing Street, and Elizabeth was on her feet. She had given a superb speech and now Campbell-Bannerman was about to reply and give his answer.

Elizabeth sat as the Prime Minister rose. The air was electric with anticipation as he began to speak but Elizabeth couldn't believe her ears. He seemed to have completely changed position. He was long-winded and dismissive, and she became more and more angry as he talked, until eventually, he concluded by saying, in a condescending manner.

"You ladies will get the vote one day, but you need to be patient."

Before she hardly realised it herself, she was back on her feet, "Sir" she cried indignantly "I have been campaigning for the vote for the last 43 years; how much more patient do I have to be?"

He looked at her and then silently rose from his chair and with one final sheepish look across at the assembled women, he left the room.

The women were incensed and rushed to Elizabeth's side complimenting her on her efforts but angry at the treatment that they had received. They were escorted from the room and through the front door. From there they marched to Trafalgar Square where a rally was taking place and Elizabeth climbed the platform to stand with Emmeline Pankhurst and Keir Hardie as they addressed the crowd to tell of the happenings at 10 Downing Street.

It was a dark day that went down in the history of the women's movement as a day of infamy and cowardice from the Prime Minister but also for the stalwart bravery of Elizabeth and her sisters.

CHAPTER 32
Treacherous Women and Emmeline Pankhurst

Elizabeth

The room was in uproar, which frankly wasn't unusual.

The women, the Suffragists and the newly named Suffragettes were disgruntled. They had seen bill after bill thrown out by skulduggery and political dirty tricks. This night they were shouting and arguing about the latest offer made by the new Liberal Government. I could feel I was losing control of the situation. I looked at Emmeline; her face displayed all the features of a fanatic. I had tried to explain to her again and again that she was going too far along a perilous road, and it was taking her at a tangent from the real issue. I could understand her concern and the thinking behind it but oh dear no, I was not going to have any part in it.

The politicians were playing a fine game, as they always do. They were offering a bill that gave the right to vote to women who were over 30 and owned property in their own name. Surprise, surprise Millicent Fawcett and Emmeline Pankhurst, both women in this category, thought it a fine idea.

I'm small, but my voice is loud: I took the floor.

"Sisters, keep the goal in your sights. We're fighting for universal suffrage, every citizen over 21 years, male and female, should have the vote; that is democracy! That is our intent and our goal. It has always been our intent and our goal we should not accept some half-way, half-baked lesser. No, no, no we want justice and equality for all."

Up she jumps, all holier than thou, Mrs Millicent Fawcett.

"Sisters, half-baked she says, well better half a loaf than no bread at all."

Up pops my honorary daughter Annie Kenney, she is no one's fool she knows how the ground lies, shouting from the back of the room as always; I am so proud of that young woman.

"That's all very well and good if you have a slice of the half a loaf we are being offered. What about us working-class lasses, no crumbs for us is there?"

They'll go with it of course, the mill girls and the pit-brow lasses will be shouted down and outmanoeuvred by the money and privilege of the devout Christian elite: twas ever thus and I am so, so, very tired of it now. If only they would keep single-minded and united behind the one cause, they would be invincible, but no they have to find side issues and then fight them to the death. It always plays right into the patriarchy's trap.

I expect it of Fawcett and Pankhurst; they would argue with themselves in an empty house, but I had hoped for better from Christabel. Disappointing but let's hope Sylvia continues with her Socialist principles and desire for social justice; she may well save the day, but sadly, that day is not now.

I am looking at yet another power-struggle. Instead of uniting and fighting the real enemy they are brawling like rats in a sack. It is an absolute disgrace, another total sell-out. I despair I really do.

In many ways Emmeline reminds me of the linnet Toby. She is a colourful and pretty bird in a tight cage. She thinks she knows what she wants, can incite the women to riot and to commit the most horrendous of crimes but she cannot think outside the cage she is imprisoned in. Unwilling to think beyond the bars of her stifling Christian beliefs and her class consciousness. She is quite willing to sell the working-class women up the river if she can gain the vote for herself and her like-minded, privileged few. She has no thought or care for anyone she perceives as below her in the social hierarchy; they are there, like poor Toby, to be used and abused as she thinks fit.

Just like Toby she sings even though the song is the song of slavery. Toby's song was a longing for freedom, but Emmeline's is a song of happy enslavement. Her Christian faith and the class system enable her to feel superior and entitled. I doubt that she will ever be free until like Toby, she gives up the ghost.

I know that she only tolerates me because she needs my brainpower and knowledge of English Law. Tisk, if that is what it takes to get justice then so be it, but I will not continue with her group of women if they are *persisting in this madness. Deeds not Words? Well, I'm all for that, I have been working hard all my adult life, but I will not condone this reckless threatening of life. Someone is going to get hurt and I have told her, but she hasn't ears to hear; no, I fear I must disassociate myself from the WSPU and its militant, criminal folly. Someone is going to die.*

Oh, Emmeline how can you have so little thought for the sanctity of life? Would that you could come to your senses and set that little bird free. Yes, you little bird, you need to find freedom, freedom of thought and freedom from your superior attitude. Truly, your money and your social standing mean nothing in the great scheme of things and if you cannot see that then your life is the poorer.

CHAPTER 33
William T. Stead
1912

"I saw my breath today."

Elizabeth looked up in surprise. "That's hardly surprising William dear, it is the middle of January after all."

"Yes, but the fact that I saw my breath means that, at least for that short amount of time, it had actually stopped raining."

Elizabeth laughed; she knew exactly what William meant. It had been another dreary wet day in a long cold January, depressing and dark. Elizabeth was really feeling her years but was always delighted and uplifted to receive a visit from her dear friend and ally, even if the weather was dire.

"Champagne Weather William, isn't that what the upper crust call it?"

"I believe they do Elizabeth; I should have brought us a case had I known it was going to be like this the whole of my visit to Congleton."

William Stead was in awe of Elizabeth, always was and always had been ever since they first met when Elizabeth, a bright, young teacher, working with Josephine Butler and his dear mother on the Contagious Diseases campaign; but now he was lovingly working hard on a biography of her life and work.

"Elizabeth dear we are growing old. We need to be sure that your work, indeed our work, is not forgotten. My biography of Mrs Butler has played a huge part in immortalising her and getting her work recognised and I intend the same for you.

I find the fact that Emmeline Pankhurst and Millicent Fawcett are held in such high esteem and you are forgotten or deliberately hidden, is most unfair and it's down to me to put that right; they are not fit to lick your boots."

"I never wear boots William" she responded lightening the moment and causing William to laugh.

"I am almost finished, and I intend to get it completed ahead of my forthcoming tour of the United States, you are well-known there and I have a couple of publishing houses already interested in the manuscript. Worry not, you will receive the acclaim that has eluded you thus far. I have always said that you are the grey matter in the brains of the women's movement, and Mrs Pankhurst has quoted me on several occasions; your story must be told. It was Julia herself that told me I must write it and she presses upon me that I must write it soon."

Elizabeth stared at him and sighed inwardly. She and William agreed on most things, the need for social justice, the need for female emancipation, and their shared pacifism; but William was an ardent Spiritualist, something that Elizabeth just could not tolerate. He had even managed to convince Annie Besant no less, a fact that amazed Elizabeth.

She knew that when William mentioned Julia, he was referring to Julia Ames, a deceased American journalist who he was convinced was his spirit guide. She found it silly and not a little disturbing. Elizabeth smiled resignedly and pointedly changed the subject.

"My archive is very important William, as you have seen I have it meticulously catalogued, it contains correspondence back to the 1850s, all of my poetry and writings, letters from senior members of the women's movement and an autobiography "Memories of a Happy Life" and of course huge amounts of Ben's writings; he was a fine poet. Frank is instructed that all this work is to be handed over to the British Library as the Wolstenholme Elmy Archive and my book is to be published after my death." She looked across to where Frank was sitting and smiled.

William looked at Frank sternly. "Young man, you have a solemn task ahead. The women of this country, nay the world, are depending on you. Your mother's work was and is crucial to the social history of this country."

Then turning back to Elizabeth, he continued. "I am committed to getting my book out by the end of the year, I want it in print while we both still occupying this planet. We are both getting rather long in the tooth Elizabeth, I feel the immediacy of the task in hand."

Elizabeth smiled benevolently and felt a modicum of peace, but the thought gave her no deep pleasure, for she felt, in her heart that ultimately, she had failed in her number one goal, she had not achieved the illusive justice she craved.

William had been to stay with Elizabeth numerous times over the last two years to talk with her about the past and to interrogate her archive. It had been a long and arduous process as William wanted to be fair and honest, feeling the need to show Elizabeth warts and all, and yet expose the amazing genius that she truly was. They had spent many long hours together as Elizabeth reminisced about her life and the many famous people she had worked with.

This wet and dreary day was his last for this visit and he had the feeling that Elizabeth's health was failing rapidly and that maybe it would be his last chance ever, so he kept pressing her and prompting her with questions.

"So, tell me Elizabeth, what of John Stuart Mill?"

"A fine man with a heart for female emancipation. His book The Subjection of Women, was a masterpiece. Of course, one of his chief influences was Harriet his wife; she was a fine sister whose heart was on fire for emancipation. I worked closely with them both in the early years. You will find a package of papers and letters in my archive, dated around 1867.

William nodded, then continued. "And what of Kier Hardy?"

"Mr Hardie was also a fine man, but of a very different character. Self-educated and extremely well-read, very active in the fight for social justice. His Free Union with Sylvia Pankhurst has caused quite a stir and not least amongst the Pankhursts themselves. Their Christian principles never extended to extra-marital activity" she cackled a laugh and her eyes twinkled. "I shared a platform with him on several occasions. Of course, he was always trying to get me to join his Party, and truth be told, I was sorely tempted, but I needed to be free of any political label; Ben joined though for a time, but of course you know that. I always pledged to work with anyone as long as they were working for the betterment of women. That was always my driving force, justice, justice, justice. Letters and papers for him are dated 1900 to 1910."

William smiled and left the room to search of the relevant information. He recognised that she was very tired, and he had kept her talking for far too long. He would leave her to take a nap before dinner.

Later, in the drawing room after dinner, William kept Elizabeth entertained with many tales of the people he had met and worked with and some of the people he had interviewed whilst researching Elizabeth's biography.

"I am on target to get this finished and I intend to take it with me on my forthcoming tour of the United States. I have two publishing houses very interested in publishing it. I just need to edit a little more and I am there."

Elizabeth smiled. "Dearest William, there is no one else I would trust to write my story than you. You stand head and shoulders above the rest for your honesty and fairness. You will do me proud I am sure, but let us not waste our last night together, tell me all about your tour and what you have on your itinerary. It was always my intention to take a trip to America but sadly, there was never the time or the finances; I am very envious."

"I have been requested by President William Howard Taft no less, to attend his Peace Congress in Carnegie Hall and I also have meetings with educators and of course, publishers. I must admit your work on your autobiography has been illuminating, to say the least. I hope I can do you justice with my poor effort."

She studied him closely, she never could believe how modest he was, even in the face of his substantial work for the betterment of women. As editor of the Northern Echo and then the Pall Mall Gazette his work had transformed journalism and both Ben and Elizabeth held him in great esteem.

His work The Maiden Tribute of Modern Babylon, and his trial, prosecution and imprisonment over the infamous Eliza Armstrong Case, had raised their deepest respect for him. He had paid a great price in his fight for the rights of prostitutes.

"So, tell me William, from where do you sail, Liverpool?"

"No Southampton and that is also the source of much excitement, for I am set to travel on The Titanic, a first-class passage no less."

Elizabeth's eyes widened in disbelief, "William how perfectly wonderful. You must keep in touch with me, I shall mark off your voyage on my globe, no I will get Frank to purchase me a map of the world and I shall stick pins in it. That way I will know exactly where you are at any given time for the whole of your adventure."

"I will send you a copy of my itinerary and the dates and towns I shall be visiting. That way you will know when the book is being discussed and can send thoughts to the Universe that it will be accepted."

"Oh no danger that it will be rejected William, your work is exemplary and much sought after. I am sure it will be in print towards the end of the year; out for Christmas I bet."

They chatted on reminiscing about past campaigns and Ben and all the other great and good people that they had encountered in their lives.

Suddenly and unexpectedly, William grew pensive and said "I hope you don't mind me asking Elizabeth but there is something that has gone through my mind many times. You and Ben were extremely close, perhaps the closest couple I have ever met, your love for each other was evident in everything you did so, does he never try to contact you from the other side?"

Elizabeth was irritated, she hated it when her friend went off on one of his Spiritualist rambles. "William dear, you know that both Ben and I do not believe in an afterlife in that sense. It is our deeply held belief that upon death we cease to exist. Human life exists in the brain and when the brain ceases to work then sadly, we are no more. We come from the life force of the Universe purely by chance and we return to the stars after our death, but not in any way that could contact us down here. The idea just does not stand up to any close scrutiny."

"I find that very sad Elizabeth as I am completely convinced of the opposite. I feel, nay I know, that we are surrounded by the souls of the departed who want to communicate with us."

They stared at each other and then Elizabeth said solemnly, "believe me William if there was contact between the living and the dead then my dear Ben would have contacted me long ago. It appears to me that spirits, apparitions and ghosts only ever appear to those who are convinced of their existence. I have a scientific mind; I only believe in that which is proven. As Ben himself used to say, "if you can't see it, smell it or touch it then it simply isn't there."

They were silent and then he said "how about we make a pact? We are both nearing the end of our tenure on this planet, let us have a secret word or phrase that only you and I know and then when such a time arrives that one or other of us crosses the veil, we will try everything in our power to make contact and prove life after death by communicating our secret word."

She stared at him and then expressed her amusement by saying. "And what will this mysterious, secret word be? It must be something that no one else could possibly know or guess, no wait, perhaps it should be a word in Esperanto?"

William's face lit up. As a fluent speaker of Esperanto this idea appealed to him greatly. "What a brilliant idea, let me think. I know that you are not as fluent as Ben was so perhaps, I should choose the word?"

"Go ahead."

William thought for a few minutes and then said "Fluo de vivo. How does that sound?"

Elizabeth frowned. "Fluo de vivo, is that stream of life?"

William was delighted. "Well done Elizabeth you are better than I thought. Stream of life it is indeed."

"Fluo de vivo, I'll remember that. I won't write it down, that would spoil your game as someone may well read it. It needs to be a proper, scientific experiment if it is to work." She smiled graciously, humouring him. "And now William I simply must go to bed. Goodnight my friend and I'll see you at breakfast."

She rose painfully from her chair, the damp January air was not good for her rheumatism, so she walked painfully towards the door and William, having risen with her took her hand, raised it to his lips and spoke "Goodnight Elizabeth, fluo de vivo my dear."

Elizabeth glared at him playfully and left the room. William followed; he was due to leave the following day and his heart was heavy, for any parting from Elizabeth was always painful but this time it had a feeling of finality that he couldn't explain.

****

The next morning brought yet more rain, but William had to steel himself and turn out, for he needed to catch the train for his journey home. After fond goodbyes with Elizabeth, he leaned forward and whispered in her ear, "fluo de vivo Elizabeth," then winked.

She laughed in spite of herself as Frank drove the Elmy's small trap out of the yard and up into Buxton Road on its way to the station. On the journey, William regaled Frank with more details of his forthcoming trip and his certainty that his book would be snapped up by the American press.

"Will there be any money in it for her?" Frank asked churlishly. "She lives hand to mouth you know; no one seems to care about her plight these days; her drawers are more patch than flannel. She and my father spent virtually all their money on campaigns for women and now she is abandoned and forgotten."

"It was a labour of love Frank, neither of them begrudged a penny. Their hearts were as big as the Universe itself and they wanted nothing for themselves. Everything they did was about justice for women and girls, but surely, I don't need to tell you that; you of all people?" He looked hard at Frank and then went on. "Don't worry she will have her share of the royalties should the book be successful. It was one of my main reasons for writing it, so I could ensure her comfort in her old age."

Frank grew quiet and looked ahead for a couple of minutes lost in his thoughts and struggling to keep his temper in check, and then he said "I'm sorry Mr Stead you must think me rude, but I am very suspicious of people's attitude towards my parents. For instance, they worked so very hard on the repeal of the Contagious Diseases Act, slaving away for many years, spending their hard-earned money and giving all the credit to Josephine Butler only for that despicable women to say that she wished to remove the stain of her association with such people as the Elmys from her character. She actually said that! You cannot deny this, you have written an extensive biography of the traitor?"

"This is all true Frank, but you mother is the bigger person, she does not bear a grudge. Whilst she may not be able to forgive, she does have the ability to move on regardless, she learned that lesson as a child. She keeps only the prize of justice before her eyes everything else is a trifle."

Frank pondered his answer for a while and then changed the subject. "Tell me more about your journey. When do you leave?"

William's demeanour changed completely, and he grew animated. "I leave on 10th April from Southampton, and I am sailing the maiden voyage of The Titanic Frank! How fortunate I am to have a first-class passage on such a magnificent ship. The President of the United States of America no less, has booked it for me. I have told your mother all about it so she can follow my journey and imagine my book being transported to the United States of America for publication."

His face was beaming, and his enthusiasm was infectious. Frank was infused by the excitement and wished with all his heart he could accompany him on his momentous trip. When they reached the station Frank helped the old gentleman from the trap and was loathe to admit that he was genuinely fond of him. He shook his hand and uncharacteristically smiled warmly as he said. "Bon voyage Mr Stead, and good luck with the book."

Thus, they parted company, Frank Wolstenholme Elmy back to his bitter boredom in Buxton House and William T. Stead to his courageous, icy death on 15th April 1912; the Titanic, his life and his precious manuscript lost forever in the frozen waters off Newfoundland.

CHAPTER 34
The Women's Suffrage March
Summer 1913

In 1913 the National Union of Women's Suffrage Societies organised a mass march. Women from all over England walked to assemble on 26th of July in Hyde Park to demand the vote. They came via several routes. One came down from the Northeast, one across from Cardiff, another across from Cornwall, one from East Anglia and yet another from Carlisle.

All along the route the women were joined by supporters, who walked some of the way with them. They called off at various towns and held rallies and gave rousing speeches. Some women walked the whole way to London and the glorious day in Hyde Park.

Elizabeth

The Women's Suffrage March is coming, I must give a speech, I must pass on the baton; throw my mantle onto the shoulders of those who can carry it into the future. They are the ones who will see the glorious day of justice. Perhaps this Olive Maud Marsh is the one to take it forward? It was she who contacted me; the organisers think I am dead already I suppose. Likewise, the Pankhursts, they have conveniently forgotten about me these days and my name has been removed. from their pamphlets and books.

Frank will try to stop me; he is getting intolerable. Trying to force me to do his bidding, keeps saying I am old and ill. When did he become such a tyrant? When did he develop such ideas?

I must admit it, he is not a pleasant man, deep, dark and capable of cruelty. Since Ben died, he seems to think of himself as the head of the house, my boss, the great patriarch! He holds the purse strings, and he is physically stronger than me; but I have my intellect, my voice and my writing and they have never let me down thus far.

I fear Frank and his motives, I don't understand where things went wrong, he has always been so very loved by Ben and I and the wider circle; or perhaps not the wider circle, he was never a very endearing child. Where did I go wrong?

Olive Maud Marsh
Journal Entry
July 8th 1913

The sun was shining brightly again today. The weather has been good to us all through this last week and yesterday's rally in Nantwich was a resounding success with lots of speeches and excited singing in the sunshine. Today however was for me, the highlight of the whole march, something really special: Congleton!

I simply could not wait; I was so excited. You wouldn't believe I am an adult woman of some twenty years; I was as skittish as a child on Christmas morning. Come on Olive, you have 10 miles to walk this morning and then a huge rally but most of all, you're going to meet "her" I told myself, my heart a flutter.

The people are so good. All along the way they have joined our ranks, given us food and drink, and accompanied us for a few miles to support and cheer us on. Some joined to head for London and the culmination in Hyde Park. This pilgrimage must draw as much attention as it can.

A few ruffians have tried to abuse us, and sadly the police have turned a blind eye, but we have devised tactics to stop them in their tracks and we are becoming well-practiced; we usually find that the local supporters do all they can to silence them.

The worst place to date was Preston, where we were joined at the borough border by a band of aggressive men and a huge group of policemen who accompanied us right through the city watching for any sign of incitement. They were very hostile and intimidating but we kept the peace and our heads and passed safely through the borough.

Liverpool was memorable. Great crowds cheered our way; huge numbers of women joined the march. A truly great city; such friendly people, despite the obvious deprivation and poverty on her streets.

News from other groups tell of great throngs of hostile men and some women. It has not been as easy a ride for everyone. The idea of female enfranchisement is one that stirs up much anger; people simply do not like the idea of change and equality.

Happily, we arrived this fine July day in Congleton in Cheshire. Tired yet excited, we rallied in the fairground, but I needed to leave them and find Buxton Road. I had been given directions and I was told that it wasn't far away. I asked a local woman for directions, and she offered to walk me there. So, we three women, Lydia Lucas, Margaret Worral and I, set off for the short walk to Buxton House.

On arrival I couldn't believe how small it was: to think that Elizabeth's worldwide campaigns had been fought from this little house. Our knocks were answered by her son Frank. Not much to say about him except, he seemed a quiet man with little to distinguish him from any of the other dull fellows that populate the planet; a disappointment on first appearance.

We were taken round the house into the garden and there she was! the famous Elizabeth Wolstenholme Elmy in all her glory: so tiny, so frail and so very, very old.

Of course, I knew her age 81, but the sight of her diminished physical power was a real shock. However, although her body was weak her mind was still razor sharp and she regaled us with some tales about her campaigns and the famous people she had met and worked with on the campaign trail.

All too quickly it was time to leave but at this point Elizabeth became agitated. She was so unhappy that she hadn't been able to make it down to see the women on the fairground and it was obvious that she wanted too so very much. Suddenly she seemed to make a decision and she turned to Frank and said, "Saddle Vixen."

Frank obviously thought this a really bad idea and said quietly "Mother you cannot be serious you are too weak; you will hurt yourself."

"Saddle Vixen" she repeated with a steely look in her eye, and it was obvious that Frank knew that what Elizabeth wanted, Elizabeth got. With a sigh, he crossed the garden to the stable and returned shortly after leading a robust but gentle little pony on the end of a leading reign.

"Come on then Mother, let me lift you to the saddle."

There was an edge in Frank's voice that caught my attention; something not quite right but my attention shifted to the plucky old woman sitting on Vixen's back. There she was, still displaying all the grit and determination that she had employed throughout her long life of campaigning. Tears were streaming down my face as we walked down Buxton Road and entered the fairground where the women were waiting to start the next leg of the march.

As gentle Vixen moved onto the fairground the women moved quickly forward to reach out to Elizabeth and to pet the pretty pony she was mounted on. One group of women pushed to the front and a dark-haired girl called out "Mrs Elmy, Mrs Elmy we are from Crewe we are Factory Girls."

Elizabeth looked across at them and her old face broke into a wide toothless smile. "Ah! Ada Neild I believe. Well done with the letter writing."

Ada was thrilled and replied, "I took my inspiration from you Mrs Elmy, you know how to write a letter or two."

"The pen is mightier than the sword Ada, always remember that. You have shown great bravery with your actions. You don't have the security of a fortune behind you, but you risked everything and paid the price. I hope you have found employment?"

" I am with the Burnley Clarion Van Mrs Elmy, we have great plans to get the vote and social justice."

Elizabeth lifted her hand in salute as Frank turned Vixen and headed up Park Lane to lead the procession on its next phase, the women singing and waving their banners behind her. She led the parade for half a mile until she reached the station and the canal bridge and there she stopped, pulled aside and watched as the women passed, dipping their banners, and throwing her kisses.

As I left her side she said earnestly, "I am handing on the baton, take it up, take up arms and get that vote."

We were both in tears now and looking at her I knew what this moment was costing her physically; this would probably be Elizabeth's very last public appearance.

It was a wonderful moment, but one thing bothered me. I caught a look on Frank Elmy's face: an unguarded moment. I cannot name it, but it was certainly not the loving look of a proud son.

We left Congleton on a high note, but I had a catch in my heart. I know I have a dim view of men, that my life story is one dogged by childhood abuse, but I must own it: I don't like Frank Elmy.

Frank

Well, I thought I'd seen the back of all that sort of rubbish but no, a deputation of women calling in on the way to London. Packing the fairground with their nonsense. My mother, the stupid old woman, insisting on getting on a horse at her time of life: if only she had fallen off the thing and broken her neck; done us all a favour.

I couldn't do anything but play the dutiful son, but that Olive Marsh woman gave me the creeps. She watched me! I could tell she was observing my every move with suspicion, I could feel the heat of her stare. I'm not used to that, I'm usually ignored, part of the furniture; I pride myself on being like those three wise monkeys, but I see all, I hear all, but I speak, not at all.

That Marsh woman looked into my soul; I was not comfortable. When are these people going to forget about my mother and leave me in peace?

CHAPTER 35
The Archive

Over the next year, Elizabeth's state of mind became more and more fragile. It was as though her weakening mind was reflecting her weakening body. There were days when she didn't recognise people or places and her confusion was upsetting to witness. Sometimes though, she was as clear and rational as ever and she spent those days looking through her precious archive of letters and papers kept so meticulously in chronological order. This was the record of her life and work, this was what was going to live on when she was gone. The delight she took in the memories these papers held, was the only thing that gave her life meaning now.

Her autobiography, "*Memories of a Happy Life*" was often re-read and edited. She had told a few close friends about the existence of the manuscript and had advised them that she wanted it published after her death. She had discussed it at length with Ben and both he and William had pressed upon her that this was probably going to be the most important thing she would ever do; this was what the historians would use to record the times they had lived through and their monumental part in charting its course. This book would be her arrow into the future.

William's death and the loss of his precious biography had caused her so much distress, she had been plunged into a deep melancholy, that grew and grew. It galvanized her to protect the precious archive all the more. She knew it was all that would live on after her demise.

****

Almost two years to the day of the sinking of the Titanic Elizabeth received a letter from William Stead's daughter Estelle. It wasn't the first, there had been a steady stream of them, reminding Elizabeth of William's writings which she claimed were prophecies. Apparently, in 1886 he had written a story that appeared to prophecy the sinking of the Titanic. She had written back that William had written constantly, and it was hardly surprising that one of his hundreds of stories would appear to be a premonition of a future event. Did the story name the ship? Did William specifically say he would be on it?

Their letters had bounced back and forth for several months, Estelle was so completely convinced that she was in constant contact with her dead parent that Elizabeth feared for her sanity.

Eventually, Elizabeth grew weary and stopped answering the letters, for Estelle was a stonewall concerning any rational argument that attempted to clarify her thoughts on the topic by giving another possible reason for what was happening. True to form Elizabeth had little truck with messages from beyond the grave although at first, she had been concerned and not a little spooked but very quickly it became apparent that the messages were nonsense and certainly didn't lead Elizabeth to conclude that William T Stead was alive on the "other side." She felt nothing but pity for Estelle, but she was old and tired and could not spare her meagre strength on such correspondence as this.

When the letter arrived, it was Frank who brought it to her but looking at the return address she said "Oh dear, poor Estelle again. Put it on my desk dear I'll read it later."

Of course, she didn't go back to it, her tired old brain had not retained the information and as soon as the letter was out of her sight, she forgot she had received it. Frank however did not forget it as he was intrigued as to what Estelle had to say, so when Elizabeth was in bed that evening, he opened it.

Mrs Wolstenholme Elmy
Buxton House
Buglawton
Cheshire

14th April 1914

Dear Mrs Elmy

I have been in contact with my father several times over the last weeks and he conveyed to me a message of great importance. He tells me that a terrible conflagration is coming upon the world and that this is the year it will commence.

He says it will be a war like no other and that many, many lives will be lost. He has impressed upon me and all present in the room, the need to prepare and take precautions. He particularly mentions your archive and the need to get it to a place of safety. Mrs Elmy he was most thorough in expressing that your archive is in great danger and that you must remove it to a place of safety, or it will be lost forever.

He also informed me that you will not believe this message is from him as you are extremely sceptical about life after death and that you believe that contact between the two worlds is impossible.

He has therefore given me a most specific message for you personally which I received on 10th March 1914 via the automatic writing of the medium Mrs Bella Lane. I must admit that the words make no sense to me or Mrs Lane but out of love for my father and knowing how important he feels this to be, I must write and pass on his message. Part of it appears to be in a foreign language but he says you will understand.

My father's message to you is as follows:

"Take care of your archive, fluo de vivo."

I hope this means something to you as my father is most insistent that I get the message to you.

Yours sincerely

Estelle Stead

More ridiculous female nonsense thought Frank as with a contorted face, he screwed up the letter and threw it on the fire.

****

October 1914
Frank

Well, she's obviously gone senile now, yet still she continues to throw her orders around and dictate my life. She really thinks that this mountain of rubbish she has spent a lifetime accumulating is of value to anyone but her. Of course, Father humoured her and added to it himself; there's quite a lot of his stuff among it. The fool! I must clear it all out.

This rubbish takes up two rooms of my house. My Archive, she calls it; she thinks more of this paper than she does of me. I'd like to see it burn. I'll get the council to clear it; I'll get it arranged tomorrow. They are asking for old paper to recycle for the War Effort. The silly old woman doesn't even realise there is a war. I'm going to really enjoy watching her face when they come to take it all away. I'll wager she starts one of her tantrums; I'll enjoy that too.

She is weak in body and mind, but I know she will still be aware that her precious "life's work" is being removed. I have waited for just the right point in her decline, weak in body and mind but still able to understand what is going on.

I will play the dutiful son as usual but, when we are alone, I will delight in telling her that it's gone and that it will be recycled for the war effort. Oh, the irony of that, the great Elizabeth Wolstenholme Elmy, pacifist extraordinaire, the great anti-war campaigner; what a hoot!

She will cry of course; she cries a lot these days. She gets moments when she thinks through the fog in her brain and is lucid and logical. It's then she understands her situation, her vulnerability and most of all, her powerlessness. So yes, I will let her fret about the loss of her papers and then when I judge she is totally clear-headed, I will tell her exactly where it's all gone. She will cry and I will laugh.

Revenge is a dish best served cold and I have waited a long time to consume this particular banquet.

****

Something was going on and she didn't understand. There were men in the house, and they were touching her precious papers and not gently either. They were gathering them up and throwing them indiscriminately onto handcarts. She needed to stop them, but this man was preventing her from doing so.

"Ben, Ben they are stealing our work. Ben, Ben where are you?"

A man is holding her back and talking in a kind, gentle voice but she does not trust him one bit, she is struggling to be free, but his strength is superior to hers.

"There, there Mother dear, all this rubbish will be removed and then you will feel much better. We can't keep it here any longer it will be harbouring vermin, and we don't want that now do we? Keep calm dear heart."

She could hear his words, could see his face but it didn't make sense. He wasn't a kind man, she knew that much, but her addled faculties could not solve the conundrum. Her brain, old and broken as it was, was giving her conflicting information.

This man was talking in a kind, soothing voice but she knew him to be harsh, angry, cruel. The words he was saying actually made no sense; he talked of being "rid" of her precious archive. She had plans for it. It was a fully documented account of her life's work and the hopes and dreams she had for the future and equality of the sexes. She didn't want to be "rid of it" she wanted to protect it from these men.

There was nothing she could do except fight. She had spent her life fighting in one way or another and she fought now with all her might, but her strength was greatly diminished and the woman who once bravely climbed onto the statue of Richard I and defied the patriarchy, was forced to watch her life's work taken away on handcarts. A cruel act of revenge by a son so bitter and dysfunctional that he lacked all compassion.

CHAPTER 36
The End of All Things
March 1918

If you were to ask Frank Elmy what it was like to have a mother like Elizabeth, he would smile shyly and say, "interesting."

However, it is unlikely you would ask Frank Elmy such a question or indeed any question at all, for he was a reclusive, withdrawn sort of chap who rarely engaged in conversation, preferring instead his own company. You would probably have found him in his precious Coop Library in Mill Street, studying some book or other perhaps on mathematics or astronomy which were two things of great interest to him.

He was known as a quiet, studious little man who, unlike his parents found public speaking not just difficult, but distasteful: he spoke little but thought a lot. A deep, unreadable character, aloof and self-contained.

To the outside world, Frank was a dutiful and loving son who spent his life alongside his parents on their many campaigns for women's rights. Very few people, if any ever penetrated the protective carapace that he had painfully constructed around himself. In Frank's case what you saw was most definitely not what you got. He was in fact, a total sham. He had constructed an outward image that he worked hard to maintain. Inside he was a bubbling cauldron of resentment and hatred.

So poisoned and poisonous was Frank Wolstenholme Elmy that a loving relationship with another human being, was totally out of the question. He couldn't look at a woman without feeling a flood of anger and hatred. Deep-seated misogyny, deeply ingrained in his psyche. He simply hated women and blamed them for all the imagined ills in his life.

Because of women he had had a miserable childhood, ignored and unloved by a woman who should have been at home looking after him but who was instead, out in the world campaigning, fighting for other women to have the freedom to do the same.

How misguided and miserable was his father, allowing and encouraging her as he did? He should have reined her in; put a stop to her antics. He was equally to blame for Frank's miserable life.

They had not given him the love and the attention he deserved and craved; they were too taken up with their all-consuming love for each other and their endless crusades for the rights of women; they had even spent his inheritance on the whole sorry debacle. He hated them both with a vengeance, but for his mother, he had a special kind of hatred. To the outside world, Frank was a loving and devoted son, a quiet, polite man, but inside he was bitter, twisted and ugly.

Elizabeth

The days are long now, and my eyes are dimmed. The days drag by so slowly and my old bones ache and cry out for comfort. With Ben gone and so many friends beneath the sod, I have time to reflect on my life and times.

I did of course write all my memories down in my book, Memories of a Happy Life, but somehow it was stolen from me: I'm not sure how that happened, I think Frank had something to do with it, but I can't remember; I only know that it is lost, and I am at a loss. It was to be my legacy for the future, but now it has been stolen and I haven't the time to write it all again and besides, all my precious papers have gone as well.

Dead people are living in my head; they are very much alive in there. They talk to me and influence my thought processes. People live as long as there are people who remember them, they say. Well, I have reached an age where there are more dead people than living, breathing walking ones.

Some days I can almost feel the cold wind of that day in Roe Green when the voices called to me from the soil, the voices of the women. Justice, they wailed, and I have tried, I have really tried. I have carried their voices in my head throughout all the battles I have fought, through the triumphs and the failures, but I have no life left to complete the task.

I suspect this is the penalty for living to such a great age. Eighty-five! I've had enough, I can feel my body closing down, wearing out; making ready to give up the ghost. I have a deep and abiding sadness; I didn't do it, I didn't achieve the ultimate prize, I didn't win the vote!

We still have not had justice. I have shot into the brown; failed miserably.

****

Elizabeth was agitated. She couldn't find a clear place in her mind that told her what was happening. Through the fog, she knew that she needed to do something really important and that this man was trying to prevent her. She left her bedroom and walked towards the top of the stairs. She could hear him behind her talking, "the man." His words registered with her as aggressive and harsh.

Was it father? No father was dead, was it Uncle George? Whoever it was she was having none of it, no man was going to tell her what to do, those days are gone. She turned at the top of the stairs and confronted him. Her sharp bright eyes fixed upon his and she rose to her full height and tried to stare him out. She watched emotionless as his face, became so contorted by anger that it was unrecognisable to her.

"You stupid old woman" Frank ground out through gritted teeth and reaching out he put his hand roughly onto her chest and pushed hard.

Elizabeth's face registered what was happening and filled with fear she lost her balance and fell backwards. Thump, bang, bang, bang, down she went head over heels down, down like a sack of potatoes her head hitting the stairs as she went. She landed in a heap, nine steps down, at the bottom of the first flight, her head making a sickening slapping sound as it hit the tiles on the landing.

There was a shocking silence as Frank looked at the heap at the bottom of the stairs. He was emotionless and empty. He slowly descended the stairway until he was beside the broken body of his mother. Bending down he felt for a pulse, although he thought it patently obvious that she was quite dead. He felt only relief: he felt no fear because he knew that no one would question the death of an 85-year-old woman who was living with dementia. No one would ask if she had been pushed, no one would suspect foul play from her dutiful, loving son. He knew quite well that no one cared about women, especially old ones.

He took several deep breaths and walked purposefully towards the front door and upon opening it, he walked out into the street to summon help. He took his time selecting which of the neighbours he would ask but eventually decided upon Mrs Ellen Bailey, who had been friendly with Elizabeth for many years. He pounded on her door and when she opened it, he made a grand show of faux distress by saying "Mrs Bailey come quickly Mother has fallen downstairs."

Ellen ran behind Frank and through the front door of Buxton House and seeing Elizabeth lying in a pool of blood, she ran to her side and fell to her knees. At first like Frank, she assumed Elizabeth quite dead, but as she placed her arms around her friend's shoulders Elizabeth groaned and opened her badly bruised eyes. Ellen could see the deep cut at the back of her head; Elizabeth stared at her in earnest and said croakily "He pushed me, he pushed me down the stairs."

Ellen sent Frank for Dr Ferns who arrived quickly and examined Elizabeth. "I think we should get her back upstairs and, in her bed" he said, and Frank swooped in with a show of deep concern and lifted her in his arms and carried her lovingly upstairs to her room. Ellen took Dr Ferns aside and spoke.

"I think Frank is at the end of his tether Doctor, I wouldn't like to trust him with Elizabeth's care here at Buxton House. I think a care home would be the best idea. She told me he pushed her downstairs."

Dr Ferns nodded "Yes, she really is not in the best of condition mentally. I'll see what I can do."

So, Elizabeth was taken to a care home in Manchester where she lived a further six weeks until she died on 12th March 1918 just a few days after the passing of the Representation of the People Act which gave the vote to women over the age of 30 who owned property.

It was not the justice Elizabeth was fighting for.

When the police investigated Elizabeth's death, Ellen Bailey told them what Elizabeth had said and was questioned closely. She reported that Elizabeth had been very difficult these last few years and Frank had probably lost his patience with her. "He had needed the patience of a saint of late. She was such a dizzy age." she said.

The police questioned Dr Ferns who told them impatiently "Mrs Elmy was 85 years old and suffering from advanced dementia, which means you cannot trust a word she said. After all, she was very old and had had a good, long life."

The inquest decided that Elizabeth had died due to an accident in her home.

Tis a thing of great sadness that a woman whose childhood had been plagued by domestic violence administered by her father and her uncle and who then went on to be a campaigner against that very same thing, a woman who received the adoration of the women of England who crowned her their Nestor, should die a victim of domestic violence at the hands of her own son.

The End

EPILOGUE

This book is a work of fiction. For the facts of Elizabeth's life, I have drawn heavily on the forensic research of Dr Maureen Wright and have kept as near as possible, to the actual timeline of events. The details about her relationships, particularly that with her son are all works of my imagination.

Little is known about Frank Elmy and his relationship with his mother, but we do know that Elizabeth's precious archive of writings including her poetry was taken away on handcarts and destroyed for the war effort in 1914. This was a grave mistake and a terrible loss, and I cannot conceive of any scenario where Frank Elmy could think it right to allow that to happen. It is unlikely that anyone else could have made that decision as by then Ben was dead, and Elizabeth was living with dementia.

Likewise, Elizabeth's death: there seems to be conflicting reports that she fell down the stairs at a care home in Manchester or that she fell at Buxton House and some hint in the evidence of the neighbour, Mrs Ellen Bailey, that Frank had been bad-tempered and impatient with her in her latter months. Again, I have used my imagination, my own experience with my own mother's dementia journey, put two and two together and made an end that gives the book its final twist.

The storyline with Emmeline Pankhurst is based on Elizabeth's letters which seem to indicate that their relationship was tempestuous, and Elizabeth did resign from the WSPU due to the militant, life-threatening tactics of the suffragettes.

The storyline with William Stead is more or less true, he was a passenger on the Titanic and did not survive, he had got the only manuscript of a biography of Elizabeth's life with him, and he was a leading Spiritualist and fellow Esperanto scholar. The last sightings of him report that he was seen swimming in the icy waters helping other passengers into lifeboats.

I hope you enjoyed the book which is written in memory of Elizabeth Wolstenholme Elmy to whom so much is owed by women both Nationally and Internationally.

Shine with the stars Elizabeth.

Susan Munro
Chair
Elizabeth's Group
2024

Team Munro

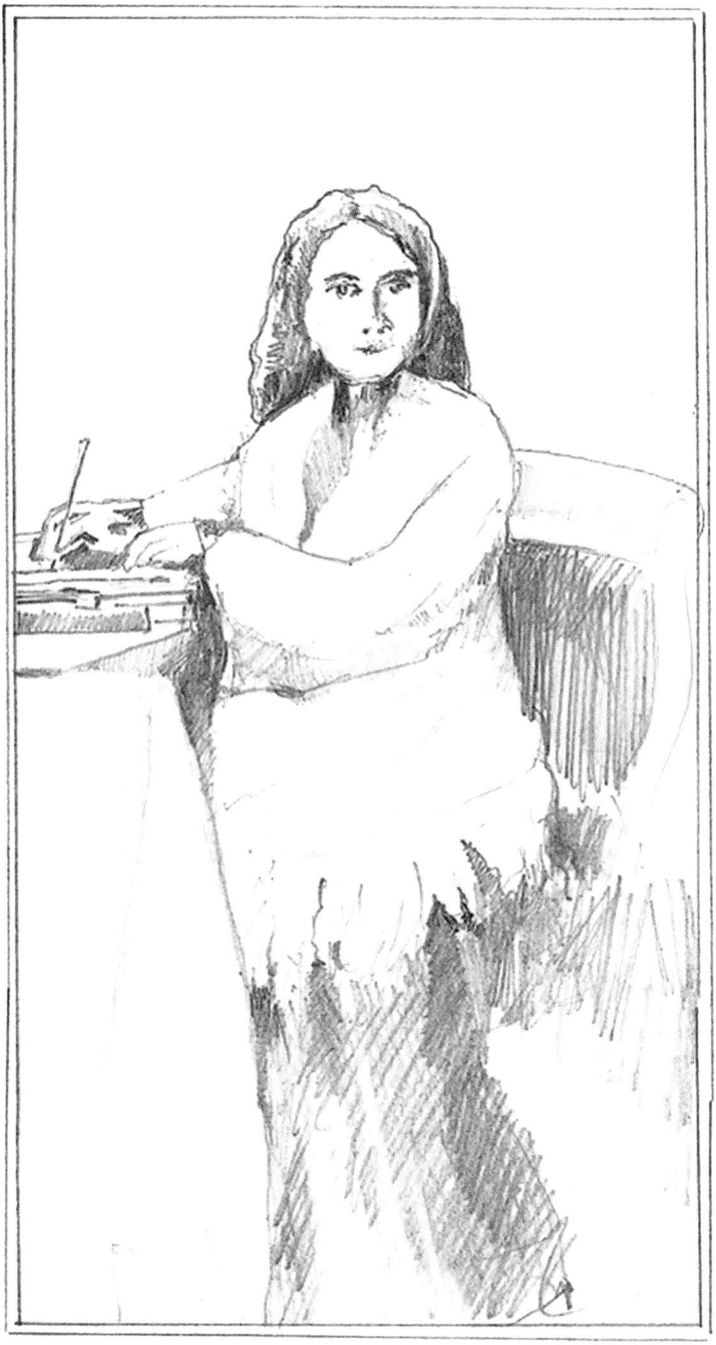

ELIZABETH'S GROUP
Registered Charity No 181256

Website
www.elizabethelmy.com

Facebook
https://www.facebook.com/elizabethsgroup

YouTube
https://www.youtube.com/@elizabethsgroup5341/featured

email
elizabethwelmy@gmail.com

ACKNOWLEDGEMENTS

Grateful thanks to all those who helped in
the production of this book.
To the good friends who read it and gave
their opinion and encouragement.
To Eliza Loftus for her stunning artwork and especially to
Jonathan Parry for his dedication and infinite patience.

Thank you each and every one.